GRIPPED
part 3

GRIPPED PART 3
THE FALLOUT

Written by Stacy A. Padula
Edited by Michael Mattes

Briley & Baxter Publications | Plymouth, Massachusetts

ISBN: 978-1735016818

Book Design: Amy Deyerle-Smith

In Loving Memory of Diana Herbig

MAIN CHARACTER BACKGROUND INFORMATION

Taylor Dunkin

Taylor was the quarterback for Northeastern University and ranked by ESPN as an NFL Top Prospect until he tore his ACL, MCL, and both menisci during a football game in 2016. He became addicted to painkillers after his second knee surgery and began dealing drugs to support his habit. He and his crime ring are currently being investigated by the Boston Police.

Marc Dunkin

Marc is Taylor's youngest brother and a senior at Montgomery Lake High School. He is committed to attend Boston College in the fall of 2018. In November of 2017, he found out that Taylor was selling drugs to Luke Davids—Marc's best friend—and that Luke was giving drugs to kids from their hometown. Marc has since set off to reverse the damage caused by Luke and Taylor.

Jordan Dunkin

Jordan is the middle Dunkin brother. He is a college sophomore, who plays football for the University of Notre Dame. Jordan was known for taking nothing seriously in high school; however, he has matured a lot in college. Marc and Jordan had a falling out during Jordan's senior year of high school over a girl they both liked—Michelle Taylor. Marc erroneously believes Jordan tried to date rape Michelle.

Chris Dunkin

Chris is the younger cousin of Marc, Jordan, and Taylor. He is a freshman at Montgomery Lake High School. His parents travel frequently for their business based in London, so Chris has grown up being very close with his older cousins, who frequently babysit him. Chris began partying at a very young age and experimented with many different drugs in middle school. Today, however, he is completely sober.

Jason Davids

Jason, like Chris, is a freshman at Montgomery Lake High. He is well known for his wit, humor, and charisma. He was in a long-term relationship with Cathy Kagelli until November of 2017. At the beginning of the schoolyear, Jason made many mistakes that he desperately wants to fix. He is determined to win back Cathy's heart.

Cathy Kagelli

Cathy is a freshman at Montgomery Lake High School, known for her beauty and intelligence. She dated Jason Davids until November of 2017 and has been seeing Marc Dunkin since December of 2017. Cathy has struggled with anxiety and depression since she and her identical twin sister, Chantal, had a falling out in 2016.

Chantal Kagelli

Chantal is Cathy's identical twin, also a freshman at Montgomery Lake High School. She is a kind hearted, devout Christian, known for her optimism. For a year and a half, she erroneously believed that Cathy pretended to be her and broke up with her middle-school boyfriend, Jon Anderson. She just found out that the breakup was a huge misunderstanding on Jon's part and that Cathy never backstabbed her.

MEET THE CHARACTERS

Top Row: Chris, Marc, Jason, & Cathy
2nd Row: Chantal, Taylor, Lisa, & Luke
3rd Row: Alyssa, Courtney, Jeff, & Bryan
4th Row: Jordan, Jon, Matt, & Ally

PREFACE

To Readers Across America:

Each day, more and more young adults fall prey to substance abuse. As an educator who works mainly with high school students, I was moved to write a book series for teenagers that shares how it happens—how good kids become drug addicts, how downward spirals start, how harmless fun can quickly turn into a life-threatening addiction.

The story told in the series is raw and realistic. I did not censor much of the content, for I believe the truth is important and powerful. In our world in which twelve-year-old kids overdose in middle school bathrooms, it is time for authors to stop sugarcoating their content to appease schoolboards. I am aware that this book may be banned by public schools because of the harsh realities portrayed between its covers. However, I did not write any part of the *Gripped* book series in hopes of it being taught in English classrooms. The truth is far too controversial for that, even though the events depicted in *Gripped* happen daily across America.

The series portrays the story of Taylor Dunkin who was an acclaimed college athlete, seemingly destined for the NFL but sidelined by injury. His depression leads him to begin abusing his pain medication and eventually become a drug dealer to support his habit. He supplies drugs to high school students from his hometown, which leads to other characters becoming ensnared. The story shows how drug abuse can skew individuals' values and change their perspectives. It follows other characters such as Luke Davids, Cathy Kagelli, Chris Dunkin, and Jason Davids (also featured in my *Montgomery Lake High* book series) whose lives have been affected by Taylor's decisions. It shows the psychological, biological, and environmental reasons behind why people often begin experimenting with drugs and how slippery the slope can be. Most importantly, this book series educates readers on how people can pick up the pieces of their lives and recover from such a horrific epidemic.

I have written five other young adult novels that address teenage social issues. They comprise the *Montgomery Lake High* book series. Over the past eleven years, the books have frequently been on the Amazon top 100 best seller list for young adult books that address substance abuse. In the fall of 2017, four of the books were top 10 best sellers within the category. Considering the sharp rise in prescription drug overdoses and opiate abuse, I feel that the *Gripped* book series is needed now more than ever. Please join me in helping to protect the youth from opiate and benzodiazepine abuse by recommending Gripped to a teenager you know.

Sincerely,
Stacy A. Padula

SCENES FROM GRIPPED PART 2

TAYLOR WAS WALKING ACROSS Northeastern's campus with his head down, hoping no one would recognize him, but nevertheless being bombarded by students who were excited to see him back at school. "I was only here for a meeting," he stated over and over again while trying to make his way back to his Jeep. Despite how popular everyone was making him feel, he felt like a failure who should have been well on his way to graduation—not discussing his transfer options.

"Taylor?" a female voice called out, stealing him away from his condemning thoughts.

He turned to his left only to see Marc's friends, Katie McKnight and Michelle Taylor, walking toward him. He lowered his eyebrows, wondering why they were at Northeastern. He had not seen either girl in over a year.

"How are you?!" Michelle cried out as she threw her arms around him in a tight embrace.

He hugged her back, finding it bizarre that he had already seen four of Marc's friends that afternoon. "Good," he replied.

When Michelle let go of him, Katie was right beside her with a hug in waiting. "It's good to see you," Katie said. "Are you back here?"

"No. I wish," Taylor replied, glancing back and forth between the two girls. He could not believe how grown up they looked. He had known them since they first became close with Marc in middle school. Realizing they would be going off to college in less than a year made him feel old. "I just had a meeting with my old advisor about something. What are you girls doing in Boston?"

"This," Michelle replied with a wide grin. "Touring colleges."

"Ah, that makes sense. Did you both apply here?" Taylor asked.

Michelle and Katie nodded.

"Co-op has made this school so popular; I don't know if I would have gotten in without football," Taylor remarked.

"Well, the nursing school might be my first choice, but Michelle has her heart set on Notre Dame," Katie informed him.

Taylor widened his eyes, startled to hear the name of the university he had once planned to attend. As he glanced at Michelle, he wondered why she would consider going to school with Jordan. According to Marc, Jordan had tried to date-rape Michelle at a party two years prior; according to Jordan, he had never laid a hand on her. Although Taylor broke up the fight between his brothers that night, he never learned the truth of what had made Michelle so sick. If Michelle was willing to attend college with Jordan, then he most likely had not drugged her.

Michelle smiled. "I have a friend on the football team who speaks rather highly of the school," she said in a lighthearted manner.

Taylor raised his eyebrows. "Jordan?" he asked.

Michelle smiled again. "He's flying home tonight to spend Easter with your family. He passed up on a trip to Punta Cana for you guys."

Taylor cocked his head to the side. "Since when do you talk to Jordan?"

"Since he came home for Christmas," Michelle replied with a sparkle in her eye.

Taylor grinned, feeling a great sense of relief and knowing for sure that his brother had not tried to force himself onto Michelle. "That's great," he said. "I had no idea Jordan was coming home."

"Oops. Sorry if it was supposed to be a surprise," Michelle apologized with a cringe. "He probably never thought I would run into you in a million years."

"It *is* strange," Taylor commented. "I haven't been on this campus in months."

"Eerie," Katie said and shuddered.

"Well, there's no school tomorrow, so a bunch of our friends are going out tonight in the Seaport," Michelle explained. "Katie and I headed in early to visit BU and here. Actually, Marc's in town, too. He has a meeting at BC."

That makes a lot of sense, Taylor thought, assuming that was why Luke and Cathy had been in the city. "Tell him to visit me," Taylor said. "I miss him."

Michelle nodded. "I will. He'll be shocked that we saw you."

"Does he know you've been talking to Jordan?" Taylor questioned her curiously.

Michelle dropped her brown eyes and shook her head. "No, not yet."

"Marc thinks Jordan drugged you," Taylor said in a low tone. "You need to set him straight."

Michelle looked up at Taylor strangely. "I told him Jordan never touched me that night."

"He thinks that's only because he and Chris barged into the room before he could," Taylor whispered and looked her directly in the eye. She seemed sincere but confused.

"I got sick, and Jordan tried to take care of me," Michelle stated. "He didn't drug me."

Taylor glanced back and forth from Michelle to Katie, observing that both girls looked uncomfortable. He wondered if Michelle even knew that Marc and Jordan were in a feud. Marc could have very well kept that to himself. He was a far more private person than Taylor or Jordan. *Jordan must have told her,* Taylor reasoned. *Jordan holds nothing back.* "Do you realize that Marc and Jordan haven't gotten along since that party?"

"That's part of the reason why Jordan's coming home," she replied. "He wants to make things right with Marc."

"I don't think talking to you is going to better his chances with Marc," Taylor said matter-of-factly. "I'm pretty sure Marc still has feelings for you."

Michelle rolled her eyes. "Marc has a new girlfriend," she said. "That's the only reason why I felt comfortable letting Jordan back into my life. Marc hooked up with a freshman in December, and he brought her to my ski house over Christmas break. They're still together."

"So, you stopped talking to Jordan a couple of years ago because of Marc?" Taylor questioned her.

Michelle nodded. "Marc is my best friend, and I saw how much it bothered him to see me with Jordan."

"He thinks you stopped talking to Jordan because Jordan drugged you," Taylor reiterated. "You need to tell him the truth."

Michelle and Katie both winced.

Taylor looked at them in a perplexed manner. "Why does it seem like you don't want to do that?"

Michelle sighed and glanced from Katie to Taylor. "*Jordan* didn't put anything in my drink that night," she stated with emphasis and eyed Taylor expectantly.

He squinted in thought, thinking back to the party, trying to remember what drugs had been circulating around that time. Molly? Liquid G? Coke? Michelle was clearly trying to tell him something.

"We should get going," Katie said and latched onto Michelle's arm while eyeing Taylor precariously. "The library closes at five today, and I really want to see it."

At that moment, Taylor realized Michelle was the only person who could fix Marc and Jordan's relationship. Hopefully, she cared enough about both of them to tell Marc the truth. While Taylor was certain Michelle had not wittingly taken any drugs, it sounded to him like something had, in fact, been put in her drink—by *someone*. Why Michelle or Katie would feel the need to protect that person's identity was beyond puzzling.

"Okay," Michelle agreed. "It was so good to see you, Taylor!" she cried and threw her arms around him again. "I'm going to fix this," she whispered into his ear.

CHAPTER 1

Aᴛᴇʀ ᴡᴀʟᴋɪɴɢ ᴀᴄʀᴏss ɴᴏʀᴛʜᴇᴀsᴛᴇʀɴ University's snow-covered campus and being bombarded by people seeming happy to see him, Taylor Dunkin reached his black Jeep Grand Cherokee. He climbed inside and started the engine, planning to gather his thoughts before driving home. He had to process not only what his former advisor had said, but also the news from Michelle.

Upon review of his transcript, Taylor learned that he had seventy-two out of ninety credits that were transfer eligible. However, his cumulative GPA was below the desired 3.0 and barely above the minimum 2.5 required to transfer at most institutions. Although he could write an essay describing how his injury had affected his performance in the classroom, without football, his chance of being admitted to a college as highly ranked as Northeastern was unlikely. He sat in amazement of how one year of bad choices could mess up a lifetime's worth of hard work. He had graduated in the top ten percent of his class and had scored in the ninety-seventh percentile on the SAT. Thankfully his SAT scores were still applicable, but his college GPA was shameful in his eyes.

His former advisor, Mr. Pearson, had recommended that Taylor enroll at BC's night school to take some courses to boost his GPA. If he took three accelerated classes during each of the summer sessions and earned A's, he could bring his transferable GPA up above a 3.0 and be back to where he used to stand academically. This gave Taylor some hope that, even if he couldn't play football, he could finish his business degree at a distinguished institution. It was going to be rather humbling to attend night school where his younger brother Marc would be a full-time student. However, Taylor knew he could not allow his pride to stand in his way.

Taylor had never expected to run into Michelle or Katie while visiting his former college. It seemed like a twist of fate, as if he was meant to know for sure that his brother Jordan had never tried to take advantage of Michelle. However, Taylor had been left wondering if Michelle still had feelings for Marc or if she was only into Jordan. How his two younger brothers had managed to entangle themselves in a love triangle while Jordan was numerous states away was beyond Taylor.

Michelle was beautiful and kind, so Taylor could understand why his brothers cared for her, but to let her come between their relationship was immature. Taylor knew Jordan had tried his best to explain himself and mend things with Marc, but Marc was stubborn—the most stubborn person in their family. He had high standards for himself and others; if anyone fell below those standards, he typically shut them out of his life. Taylor could not help but wonder if Marc realized resentment was keeping him from discovering the truth about what had actually happened to Michelle.

Taylor pulled his phone out of his pocket and plugged it into his charger before beginning his ride back to Southie. As he was driving, he noticed that his radio, which displayed text alerts and missed calls, said he had a missed call from Marc. Taylor's heart leaped in his chest. He immediately wondered if Marc had called him by accident but then noticed the screen also showed he had a voicemail. As he hit the button to play the message, he felt nervous. Had Cathy told Marc she had seen him? Had Marc called to berate him for selling more drugs to Luke?

Upon playing the message, Taylor was stunned to hear that Marc wanted to visit him and relieved that Marc did not sound angry. It brought Taylor immense comfort to hear his brother's voice, so he immediately called him back. His heart pounded in his chest as he waited for Marc to answer.

"Hello?" Marc's voice rang through Taylor's Bluetooth radio a moment later.

"Hey, I just got your message. Sorry, I was in a meeting at Northeastern when you called," Taylor replied, hoping the news would please his brother.

"Oh," Marc commented, sounding surprised. "Well, I'm in the city, and I wanted to stop by your place if you're around."

"I'm heading home from campus right now," Taylor informed him. "I'll be home all night."

"Where do you even live?" Marc asked.

"In a condo on Broadway in Southie," Taylor replied. "I'll text you the address. What time do you want to come by?"

"Well, I'm heading to dinner now, but I can come over after. We're going to Maggiano's, and a family-style dinner there isn't quick. I could probably get to your place by seven. I can't stay too long because I have tickets for the Bruins game."

"You'll miss first period if you come at seven," Taylor reasoned.

"It's fine. We just got the tickets last minute."

"Okay, well, I'll see you in a couple of hours then," Taylor stated happily.

"Sounds good. I'll call if I have any trouble finding it."

"All right. Later," Taylor said before ending the call. Marc did not sound upset, so Taylor doubted Cathy or Luke had mentioned anything about their visit. Before Taylor reached his condo, a call came through from his father. He answered, assuming his dad was calling about Easter.

"We're going to church at eleven and then eating around two," his father said. "Jordan's flying in tonight, and everyone wants to see you."

"I would say except for Marc, but he's actually coming by my place later," Taylor stated.

"He is?" his father asked, sounding surprised.

"Yup. I don't know why, but he's coming over before the Bruins game."

"He had a meeting at BC today. Maybe he has some good news to share with you."

"I doubt he'd care to share any good news with me," Taylor remarked. "Maybe Chris put him up to it. Chris called earlier and invited me to his house for Easter."

"You should come," his father stated. "We're your family, and we want to support you while you fix things."

Taylor sighed. "I know. I'm just embarrassed."

"Of who you were, not who you are today."

"That's not true; I hate where I am today."

"It's a lot better than where you were when I found you on your bathroom floor."

"True. I met with my advisor at NU today. If I take classes full time this summer at BC's Woods School, I'll have enough credits to transfer somewhere as a senior."

"That's great, T," his dad said. "When can you enroll?"

"Summer classes start in May, so I should register soon."

"I know you haven't asked, but we'll obviously pay your tuition."

"No," Taylor stated firmly. "You've already given me money for rent, and I have money in the bank. I can pay for my summer classes. You guys can pay if I actually get into a college without a scholarship."

"You belong back on the field," his father said. "I'm praying you get that opportunity."

"Me too," Taylor said. "At least Jordan is being productive. When I was his captain, I honestly questioned if he cared enough about the game to succeed at it. He's matured a lot since high school."

"Yup, Jordan pulled it together," his father said. "I can't say we're not proud, but you're the one with the gift."

"Yeah, well, a gift doesn't get you anywhere if you let yourself get sidetracked."

"Very true," his father remarked. "We're picking Jordan up at the airport tonight. He'd like it if you came home for Easter. He's coming home to see you."

"Me and the girl he likes," Taylor commented.

"Oh, did you talk to him?"

"No, I ran into her at Northeastern. She was on a college tour—Marc's friend, Michelle."

Mr. Dunkin laughed. "Leave it to your brother to have the pick of the litter at Notre Dame but still need to one-up Marc. I know Michelle; Marc's loved her since he hit puberty."

"Well, thankfully that's a mess I have nothing to do with. I'll consider coming home on Sunday based on how things go with Marc tonight."

"I'm surprised he called you," his father admitted. "I've been telling him to for months, but he's so darn stubborn. He'll forgive you in due time. He just has a hard time letting go of the past."

"I think I do too," Taylor said.

"*You* need to forgive yourself for what happened last year," his father admonished him. "Maybe once you forgive yourself and spend some time with our family, Marc will follow your lead."

Taylor knew his father was speaking with wisdom; he did need to forgive himself. That would have been a lot easier with Marc's support. He loathed himself for ruining their relationship.

"Marc told us about some of the things Chris got into last year. I'm sure there's more to it than what he told us, but Chris is doing great now. Uncle Mike and Aunt Jen are responsible for his issues. Don't carry that on your shoulders. They need to get their priorities straight. Their daughter has slipped up and called your mother 'Mom' on a few occasions. We have no problem babysitting Katie, but she's twelve-years-old, and she needs her parents. Chris is lucky to have grown up with you, Jordan, and Marc like brothers."

"I'm proud of Chris," Taylor stated. "He's a lot smarter than I ever thought."

"He tapped into the greatest power on Earth. It's the strength that has kept me on the straight-and-narrow for over fifteen years. Let it get a grip on you, and you'll see doors open that no man could ever shut."

Fifteen minutes later, Cathy Kagelli was sitting between Luke Davids and Marc Dunkin at a booth inside Maggiano's. As excited as she was for a cheese-filled Italian feast, she was nervous about spending time around Michelle. As Marc's only ex-girlfriend, Michelle was still on his pedestal. Moreover, she was the most beautiful girl at Montgomery Lake High; Cathy felt small in comparison.

According to Marc, Michelle was his best friend, someone he looked out for and loved like family. He claimed to no longer have romantic feelings for her, but Cathy could not understand how that was possible. Michelle was the closest thing to "perfect" Cathy had ever seen. She was a virgin with rock-solid Christian morals and an interest in helping others. On top of that, she was humble, warm, and smart.

As soon as Michelle entered the restaurant's dining room, Cathy planted her eyes on her long chestnut-brown hair. Michelle's friend, Katie McKnight, was also very pretty with dirty-blonde hair and a stunning smile.

"Marc, you will not believe who we ran into today!" Michelle exclaimed as soon as she reached the table. "Hi Luke. Hi Cathy."

"Shells! Katie!" Luke exclaimed and stood up to hug them.

"Hi," Cathy responded shyly.

Marc laughed. "Who did you see?"

"Taylor!" Michelle replied. "At Northeastern. He looks great!"

Marc's facial expression grew a bit tense at the sound of Taylor's name. Cathy found it rather ironic that everyone at the table, aside from Marc, had seen his brother that day. She was dreading the ride to South Boston before the Bruins game. Knowing herself all too well, she feared her conscience would get the best of her and that she would tell Marc that she had seen

Taylor. As much as she hated keeping it from him, she was afraid telling him would stop him from seeing Taylor. After realizing that Taylor was sober and considering going back to college, she wanted Marc to make amends with him. She knew, firsthand, what it was like to have a drug takeover your personality and how important it was to have people to rely on while trying to get sober.

CHAPTER 2

8 Months Prior – July of 2017

THROUGHOUT THE JULY BEFORE his freshmen year of high school, Chris Dunkin continued to spend time with Courtney Angeletti, his cousin Marc, and the older kids. The more time he spent with them, the less dependent he felt on drugs. It did not take long for him to begin developing feelings for Courtney, and he wondered if he was rebounding. Courtney appeared to have similar feelings for him because every time Chris flirted with her, she flirted back. Chris realized he needed to tell Courtney's ex-boyfriend, Bryan Sartelli, that he had been spending time with her because there was a chance they could end up dating.

As expected, Bryan was stunned to learn that Courtney had taken an interest in Chris. Moreover, he was upset that Chris had hidden it from him all month. "I'm sorry, guy," Chris apologized over the telephone in a heartfelt manner. "I didn't expect us to keep hanging out, but I'm trying to surround myself with sober people right now. Spending time with Courtney has been really good for me. I'm trying to clean up my act."

"I get why you're spending time with her; I'm just shocked she pulled you into her world," Bryan expressed. "Courtney's friendly, but she doesn't open up to just anyone."

"We connect," Chris admitted. "I'm sorry if that bothers you. I don't mean it in a physical way. I don't know what it is, but I need to keep her in my life as a good influence."

"Just don't tell me anything about it," Bryan said. "Do what you have to do but don't mention her to me. I need to clear my head of her."

"Fine," Chris agreed. "I don't blame you for being mad at me."

"I'm not mad at you."

"You should be."

"I can't control what she does," Bryan said. "I introduced the two of you. It is what it is."

"I had nothing to do with why she broke up with you," Chris assured him. "She didn't reach out to me until after you guys broke up."

Bryan sighed. "If you say so."

"I promise that I did not talk to her until you two were broken up," Chris stated earnestly, "but I understand if you resent me for it."

"I don't resent you; I resent her," Bryan said dryly. "I just need some time to get her out of my head before school starts back up. Seriously, don't tell me another thing about her."

Chris felt guilty when he hung up the phone that night. Bryan was in love with Courtney, and Chris was about to make a move on her. That made him the horrible friend he had always considered himself to be. However, he felt his sobriety was more important than being a good friend. Courtney brought something into his life that had always been missing. It was nothing like the physical connection he shared with his ex-girlfriend Lisa. He couldn't pinpoint exactly what his connection with Courtney was based on, but he knew it was unique.

The following night, when he went to hug Courtney goodbye, he kissed her on the cheek. She reciprocated immediately, so Chris hugged her extra tightly. Before letting her go, he picked her up off the ground and spun her around in the middle of her foyer. Courtney laughed as she clung to him.

"Thanks for another great day," Chris said cheerfully after setting her back on her feet.

She stepped toward him and hugged him again. "You don't have to thank me, silly," she said quietly.

He hugged her back and kissed the top of her head.

When she let go of his embrace, she looked up at him and smiled. "Will you come back over tomorrow?"

Chris nodded. "I'll try to get a ride from Marc or Jordan," he said, assuming one of his cousins would be available to drive him.

"Great!" Courtney cried. "Do you want to invite Jason and Cathy?" she asked.

"Um, we can if you want," Chris stammered, doubting Cathy and Courtney would ever become friends. When they had hung out earlier that month, Cathy had been completely aloof. Chris assumed she was upset with Courtney for hurting Bryan and, perhaps, even upset with him for spending time with her. Afterward, Chris had decided to keep as much space between Cathy and Courtney as possible. Cathy's coldness toward him and Courtney was something he had not anticipated, and he could not help but wonder how much had been brought on by resentment and how much of it had been caused by the Xanax she had been taking. He had always gotten along well with Cathy, so the change in her demeanor was not only surprising, but also concerning.

"I'd like to get to know Cathy better," Courtney expressed. "I want to know all your friends."

"I'll call people when I get home and see if anyone will be around tomorrow."

"Sounds good!" Courtney exclaimed and showed Chris to the door.

He was only outside for a moment before his older cousin Jordan pulled up in his yellow Jeep Wrangler. "Little D!" he yelled out the window. "I can't believe I'm picking you up at the mayor's house!"

Chris laughed as he hopped inside the vehicle.

"Good job, buddy!" Jordan exclaimed and gave Chris a high-five.

"Thanks, and thanks for the ride."

"No problem."

Chris loved having Jordan home from college. Even though Chris had been spending a lot of time with Marc, he still felt closer with Jordan. Jordan had stayed in Indiana until the end of June for an internship, so he had only been home for a few weeks. Chris wanted to spend as much time as he could with his cousin before he returned to college. "Are you staying at my house next weekend or is Marc?" Chris asked on the drive across their town.

"I'm not sure yet," Jordan replied. "Taylor isn't," he added.

"How is he?" Chris asked. "I haven't seen him in months."

"Not good, buddy. He's avoiding our family for a reason."

"Is he messed up on coke?"

"No, painkillers. His doctor prescribed him way too high of a dose or something. He's, like, high all the time."

"Seriously?"

"Seriously. I don't know if it's his surgeon or his regular doctor, but he's getting pills from somewhere, and they're not Perc-5s."

"So, he's prescribed too high of a dose and getting high because of it?"

"He said he wasn't high, but I know the signs. He should know the signs, too. We were taught all about them in Al-Anon. Either he's in denial, or he's trying to hide it."

"Geez. Opiates are nothing to mess with," Chris stated—stunned that Taylor would be so reckless. "Marc must have told you about what happened to me in the spring. I hope I never touch a painkiller again."

"Marc and I hardly talk, but Taylor told me."

"Well, that's ironic. What did he say?"

"He asked me to look out for you this summer because he didn't want you getting into benzos."

"Wow. Typical. *He's* high, telling *you* to look out for *me*?"

"Yup."

"Well, I haven't touched an opiate or a benzo since I ended up going to the hospital, so if you're going to worry about anyone, worry about T."

"He's going to go through withdrawal once his prescription runs out. Then he'll realize he's addicted."

"You think he really doesn't know?"

"I think the injury, depression, and drugs have messed with his head enough that there's a chance he doesn't."

"C'mon. You can tell when you're high."

"Honestly, I've never taken a painkiller. I have no idea what it feels like."

"Seriously? You've never taken a PK?"

"Nope—nothing aside from weed," Jordan stated matter-of-factly. "I don't need any drugs stronger than that."

"C'mon. You've done more than that."

"I tried molly my senior year, but I haven't touched it since I went off to college," Jordan replied. "School's tough. Football's grueling. I can't risk messing up. ND is not an easy school. They don't cut me any slack just because I'm on the football team."

"Wow. I mean, that's great. I'm just surprised."

"I joined a Catholic association, and there are rules we have to abide by," Jordan added.

Chris glanced at him strangely.

"It's a good thing," Jordan assured him.

"I knew you'd be fine," Chris stated happily. "Marc thought you'd get kicked out. Taylor said you would be competitive enough to pull it together when you needed to, but I knew you'd do all right from the start."

"I want a starting position on the roster. That's not going to happen if

I get sidetracked like Taylor. He did drugs before he even got hurt. When I went to visit him at NU, his friends offered me coke. I was in high school!"

"Did you do it?"

"No!" Jordan cried. "I've never done coke. Knowing that Taylor did it was enough to keep me away from it."

"Really?!" Chris questioned him. He knew Jordan was typically an open book unless he was playing a prank on someone, so he was likely being honest. However, Chris had always assumed Jordan partied harder than anyone else in their family because of his fun-loving and carefree personality.

"My whole life, my parents have put Taylor on a pedestal," Jordan stated. "He got arrested, and they still sang his praises. Now, he has a drug problem, and they won't believe it. Marc and I both told them that we think Taylor's overmedicated. They 'trust him to use wise judgment.' It's bullshit. I realized a long time ago that following his path would get me nowhere good."

"I'm starting to see that," Chris admitted. "It took me long enough, but I've finally realized there's more to look forward to in life than partying all the time."

"Stay away from pills—all of them. Don't mix alcohol with any other drugs—not even weed. Getting high when you're drunk gives you the spins. It's not fun," Jordan stated with a short laugh. "It's one or the other for me, and I don't touch weed during football season."

"You don't smoke every day?"

Jordan shook his head. "Nope. College is not like high school, buddy. At least not the school I'm attending."

"Your parents must be impressed by now. No?"

"I think they're too worried about Taylor's knee to notice what I've been up to."

"That can't be true. You even started in a couple of games last season. You'll start this fall. You were on national TV! Pulling off good grades at one of the best schools in the country can't mean nothing to them."

"I'm sure they're proud," Jordan commented carelessly.

"Marc is so wrong to think of you as the black sheep of the family," Chris stated. "The black sheep is definitely me or Taylor."

"He said that?"

"Yeah, last year—way before you left for college."

"He just hates me because of Michelle," Jordan said matter-of-factly.

"Oh! I saw her recently! She's good friends with Courtney's sister."

"Oh, Day?"

"Yeah."

"Cool. I guess Day's toned it down if she's close with Michelle again."

"Why? Was she a bit wild?" Chris asked.

Jordan nodded. "Big time. Typical 'politician's kid rebellion.' She partied with my grade, hardcore, when I was a senior. She loved club drugs."

"Hmmm. Surprising. She's completely straightedge now."

"That's probably a good thing," Jordan remarked. "How's Michelle?"

"Gorgeous," Chris replied immediately and then laughed. "You should reach out to her while you're home."

"No, I can't," Jordan said and let out a heavy breath. "She ended things with me. I have to respect that."

"Why'd she stop talking to you?"

"Marc, I'm guessing," Jordan replied. "They're close. She didn't want to hurt him by being with me. That's my theory."

"He still thinks you tried to date-rape her," Chris said, hoping his cousins would get to the bottom of the mess sooner rather than later.

Jordan rolled his blue eyes and shook his head. "That's insane. I never even made out with her."

"How did she end up sick that night?" Chris asked.

"That's for her to tell you, not me. I didn't put anything in her drink. Marc is disillusioned by his feelings for her."

"You and Marc really need to work things out. It's dumb."

"I've tried," Jordan said flatly. "He doesn't want to believe me because that would mean he'd have to accept that Michelle liked me. His pride won't allow him to do that."

"She hasn't tried to help you guys work it out?"

"She probably doesn't even know we're in a fight. I have no idea what she told him about that night, but if she told him why she got sick, then he wouldn't think I tried to date-rape her."

"So, you know why she got sick?" Chris questioned him.

Jordan nodded.

"But Marc thinks you drugged her?"

Jordan nodded again.

"Why don't you just tell him the truth?"

"It's not my place to say anything," Jordan replied and shook his head.

"So, all I need to do is get Michelle to tell Marc why she got sick, and then he won't hate you?" Chris asked.

"Hopefully," Jordan said, "but I'm sure he could find some way to blame me."

Chris cocked his head to the side in thought, wondering what Michelle had done to make herself so sick. He honestly could not remember too much from the party, aside from asking Lisa to be his girlfriend—oh, and dancing in front of everyone with Jordan and Marc to Britney Spears. It was hard to believe that almost two years had passed since the event. "Why are you covering for a girl who won't even speak to you?" he questioned Jordan.

"Because a part of me hopes I'll get another chance with her."

"Really?! Even after going away to college and nailing a ton of girls, you're still into Michelle?"

Jordan laughed. "*Especially* after going off to college and hooking up with a bunch of girls. The more you're out there, the more you appreciate the value of someone like MT."

"Wow. I had no idea she was still on your radar. How many girls have you been with since she stopped talking to you?"

Jordan shrugged.

"Seriously... probably at least twenty, right? Thirty?" Chris questioned him.

Jordan laughed. "I don't kiss and tell, but you're making me out to be a porn star or something, Little D."

"C'mon, girls love you. I've seen you go to bed on multiple occasions with more than one."

"You've seen too much for a fourteen-year-old," Jordan remarked.

"Probably," Chris admitted.

"High school was epic, and I'll always look back on my time at MLH favorably," Jordan said, "but in the grand scheme of things, it's a steppingstone. God help me if my greatest achievement in life is being crowned Homecoming King."

Chris laughed. "You and Marc would get along so well now. He has such a false understanding of you."

"I just hope one of us can help Taylor because he's in deep. My dad has drilled in all of our heads that addiction runs in our family, so I can't fathom why Taylor agreed to take such a high dose of Percocet. I'm sure having two surgeries was extremely painful, but there's no reason to still be on meds this many months later."

"Tearing your ACL, MCL, and both menisci sounds pretty excruciating," Chris said, "so I can see why he took the pills to begin with, but if he's still taking them, then he has a problem."

"Oh, he has a problem," Jordan stated assuredly. "Does he want to fix the problem is the real question. From what I've heard, opiate detox is not fun—lots of puking and pooping."

"How long has he been on Percocet?" Chris asked.

"I think since he got hurt in September."

"Geez. That's close to a year!"

"You should have seen him. He was so high that his eyes were rolling back in his head when he was trying to carry a conversation with me," Jordan described. "It was one of the saddest things I've ever seen. I called him out on it, and I couldn't believe he lied to me. Taylor was always arrogant, but he was never a liar."

"Drugs change people," Chris said matter-of-factly.

"He might even be on something stronger than Percocet at this point, or he could be snorting it. He looked strung out."

"T would never touch heroin!" Chris cried.

"I think he loves his body too much to ever stick a needle in it, but he could be snorting it."

"You think there's a chance he's snorting *heroin*?" Chris questioned him in utter shock.

"I doubt he's there yet, but I think he's probably snorting Percocet... or something. What I saw last weekend was not what someone looks like when they're on five or ten milligrams of Percocet."

"You have to tell your dad!" Chris exclaimed.

"I've tried. Marc's tried. Every time Taylor sees my parents, he appears to have his act together, so they don't believe us."

"Why would either of you lie about that?!" Chris asked, finding it odd that his aunt and uncle would think Marc and Jordan were being dishonest.

Jordan let out a short laugh. "They think we are overly concerned and exaggerating. They've brought it up to Taylor, and he's denied abusing his pills. My parents don't want to see it. Taylor's their pride and joy in life."

"Jordan, he could die!" Chris exclaimed, feeling a sense of urgency. "We need to help him!"

"*I'm* going to try to help him. *You* need to stay away from him."

Chris sighed. If Taylor was abusing opiates, he was one of the last people Chris should spend time with. "I get it," he mumbled.

"If Marc didn't hate me, we could team up and do an intervention," Jordan said.

"I'm sure Marc would put aside his feelings to help Taylor."

"Well, then he needs to do it fast, because I'm leaving in a couple of weeks to go back to school," Jordan said. "Between my internship and football practice, I don't have much of a summer break."

Chris sat in awe that Jordan was talking to him about a college internship and a Catholic association while Taylor was high on opiates. *Who would have ever thought things would turn out this way? Taylor—the one voted most likely to succeed—and Jordan—the "black sheep"—fulfilling each other's destinies?* Chris was happy that Jordan was making the most of his opportunities at Notre Dame, but he was devastated about Taylor.

CHAPTER 3

THE FOLLOWING AFTERNOON, CHRIS brought Jon Anderson with him to Courtney's house—after spending a half hour convincing Jon that Bryan would not get upset with him.

"I'm so glad you could come over today, Jon!" Courtney exclaimed as she greeted him and Chris inside her foyer. She wrapped her arms around Chris in a warm embrace; then she hugged Jon. "I hope you guys like volleyball because we're going to play in a tournament this afternoon."

"I love volleyball," Jon said as he and Chris followed Courtney through her finely finished foyer. "Who are we playing against?"

"A few of my sister's friends are on their way over," Courtney replied. "Once they get here, we'll split up into teams."

"Sorry Alyssa couldn't come with me today," Jon said. "She already had plans with Cathy and some other girls."

"Oh, I've met Cathy," Courtney said nonchalantly as she opened a sliding glass door that led to her enormous backyard equipped with a patio, pool, volleyball net, tennis court, basketball court, and firepit.

"Wow! You have a better backyard than Jason!" Jon exclaimed.

Courtney laughed. "I guess it pays to be in politics," she remarked as she headed over to the volleyball court. "Let's practice."

Courtney, Jon, and Chris tossed a volleyball around for a few minutes before her sister Day and Day's boyfriend John came outside with Katie McKnight. Katie had been at Chris's party the night Michelle got sick, so he wondered if she would be able to shed some light on the situation. Chris's conversation with Jordan from the previous night had given him a lot to consider. To say he was worried sick about Taylor was an understatement. The sooner Chris could get Marc and Jordan to be amicable, the sooner they could unite and help their brother.

As the afternoon went by, Jon and Courtney became much better acquainted. It was no surprise to Chris that they got along well because they possessed similar values. He was thankful that Jon was back to himself and that his rebellious stage had only lasted a few months. He hoped if Courtney became a part of their clique, she would be a positive influence on the other girls.

CHAPTER 4

Cathy Kagelli, Alyssa Kelly, Lisa Ankerman, and Leslie Lucus were having a girls' day at Lisa's house when they decided to walk to the mall. Jason and his brothers were planning a party for the upcoming weekend, so Lisa had offered to buy her friends new outfits to wear with some of the money from her inheritance.

"What are you going to do if Chris shows up at Jay's on Saturday?" Cathy questioned Lisa as they began their two-mile walk to the plaza.

Lisa shrugged.

"That's a good point," Leslie chimed in. "How would Jeff feel around Chris?"

Lisa sighed. "He's probably not coming."

"Who? Chris or Jeff?" Alyssa asked.

"Jeff. He doesn't want to make things weird for anyone. I think he's going to make plans with Andy," Lisa replied.

"That's a relief," Cathy admitted. "I love Jeff, but it would be awkward to hang out with him *and* Chris."

"For me especially," Lisa muttered. "I don't even want to think about it." She turned to face Cathy. "How do you feel about Jay drinking?"

"Luke forced him to drink at Saquish," Cathy responded defensively. "He didn't even want to do it."

"Okay, but he drank with Bryan the other night," Lisa reminded her.

Cathy rolled her green eyes and flipped her wavy auburn hair over her shoulder. "He was just trying to cheer him up. Bryan's heartbroken right now, and someone's not making the breakup any easier."

"Courtney?" Lisa assumed and raised her perfectly shaped eyebrows.

"It's more complicated than that," Cathy stated, hoping Lisa would not push the issue. "I can't get into it or Jay will get mad at me."

"Okay, wait," Alyssa spoke up. "Jon told me he was going to spend the day at the Angelettis' house with my brother. He invited me, but I already had plans with you guys. I didn't think anything of it until now. Could my boyfriend be hanging out with Courtney? I just thought he was going to hang out with John and Day."

"Probably," Cathy replied, happy that her friend had connected some of the dots. Personally, she thought Chris was being a horrible friend to Bryan, but Jason felt differently.

Alyssa gasped. "Is Jon backstabbing Bryan by becoming friends with Courtney?"

Cathy shook her head. "No. Believe it or not, Jon's not to blame for *this* mess."

"Good," Alyssa said with a sigh of relief.

"If Jay would get mad at you for telling us, then it must have to do with his brothers or Chris," Lisa reasoned. "Jay's only protective of *you* and *them*."

Cathy let out a nervous laugh. "I can't say anything. I'm sorry."

"Is Chris over me?" Lisa asked, sounding panic-stricken.

"Not a chance," Cathy replied immediately.

"Okay. Good," Lisa stated flatly.

"Are *you* over *him*?" Cathy asked.

Lisa shot Cathy a dirty look.

"What?" Cathy questioned her defensively.

"You know how I feel about Chris," Lisa snapped.

CHAPTER 5

ON SATURDAY, CATHY INVITED Lisa, Alyssa, and Leslie to get ready at her house for Jason's party. Dressed in their new outfits, all of the girls looked beautiful. Lisa's long mocha hair flowed straight down her back to her waist; Leslie's wavy blonde hair was gathered on top of her head in a loose bun; Alyssa's dirty-blonde locks were loosely curled at the bottom; and Cathy's auburn hair was scrunched into beach-waves. Mrs. Kagelli dropped the girls off at Jason's home a half hour before the party was supposed to begin. Cathy had specifically planned that so her mother would not know the party would be taking place.

Chris arrived shortly after the girls without Courtney. He was wearing a navy-blue Polo shirt, khaki shorts, and a Red Sox hat. As cute as he looked, the sight of him bothered Cathy. She wanted to tell him off for hurting Bryan, but Jason had begged her to keep quiet.

"Hi," Lisa said quietly to Chris when their eyes met.

Chris's blue eyes grew large. "Hey!" he exclaimed and leaned forward to hug her. Her whole body stiffened when Chris embraced her. "How have you been?" he asked after letting her go.

"Fine," Lisa replied and looked down at the floor.

Cathy perceived sorrow in Chris's eyes, and her feelings of annoyance toward him turned into sympathy.

"Cathy, come here," Jason said and pulled her away from their friends.

"What's up?" she asked, peering into his aquamarine eyes. *You look gorgeous*, she thought. His black hair was spiked up the exact way she liked, and he was dressed nicely in a linen shirt and designer jeans.

"Did you take Xanax before coming here?" he inquired.

Cathy shook her head. "I don't have any left. I was hoping to get some from Luke tonight."

"I baked a batch of cookies earlier. Do you want to eat one instead?"

Cathy looked into Jason's blue eyes and noticed that his pupils were dilated. "How many cookies did you eat?"

"I had a few," he admitted.

"Maybe, but I still want to get Xanax from Luke. I won't take it tonight."

Jason looked disappointed. "What if I could get you edibles more often? Would you eat them in place of taking Xanax?"

Cathy cocked her head to the side in thought. Despite the fact that her boyfriend was stoned, she could tell he was worried about her. "Do you think I'm addicted to Xanax?"

"No," Jason replied and shook his head. "I don't think you are, which is why I want you to stop taking it while you still can. I've been wracking my brain, trying to figure out a way to help you, and I asked Luke if his connection could get edibles. The problem is you would have to refrigerate them."

"Well, I obviously can't do that!" Cathy cried. "My parents or sisters could eat them by mistake."

Jason sighed. "Can you get a fridge for your room?"

"Um, that would be a little suspicious. Don't you think?"

Jason shrugged. "Ugh, I don't know. I could buy it for you as a birthday present or something."

"My birthday was three weeks ago, and my parents know you bought me a Claddagh ring."

"I don't care," Jason stated. "I want you to transition away from benzos, and I think edibles would be a great option. They make gummy worms that taste pretty good, and you would only need to eat, like, a quarter of one to feel relaxed. They're made from medicinal marijuana, so they're extremely potent."

Cathy lowered her eyebrows. "How much are they?"

"It doesn't matter," Jason said carelessly. "I'll buy them."

"Jay, my parents would think it was weird if you bought me a refrigerator," Cathy said matter-of-factly.

"Well... what if you kept them in a cooler in your closet?" Jason suggested.

"That's not a bad idea," Cathy remarked. "No one would notice if I took icepacks out of the freezer."

"Okay, so why don't you do that? Do you have a cooler?"

"No."

"I'll bring one over the next time I come to your house. I'll fill it with freeze pops so your parents won't think it's weird."

"You never cease to come up with good ideas," Cathy remarked.

"I'll have Luke get you a bunch," Jason said, "but you've got to start out eating tiny pieces. They're wicked strong."

"Okay," Cathy agreed. "I'll try them and see if they help. I can tell you're really freaked out about Xanax."

"I am," Jason admitted. "It's stealing your personality."

Cathy searched Jason's eyes. "Do you still love me?"

"Of course I do," Jason replied immediately. "I wouldn't be so concerned if I didn't."

"But if I've changed that much, how can you still love me the same?"

"Because I'm in love with *you*—the person I know is still inside of you," Jason expressed. "I just miss her; that's all."

Cathy winced. "I'm sorry," she said and put her head down. "I'm not trying to hurt you."

"You told me you were less attracted to me when I'm high, but do you think that could have anything to do with your feelings being numbed by Xanax?" Jason questioned her.

"It could," Cathy said with a shrug. "I'm still more attracted to you than anyone else. I just don't feel strong impulses to hook up with you anymore."

Jason looked positively disturbed by her confession, and Cathy felt bad. She knew it was important to be honest with him, but she feared she might have been a bit too transparent. "It probably is the Xanax," she added.

"That makes me so sad," Jason expressed. "We have such a strong connection. Please don't let drugs steal that away from us."

The sadness she saw in his eyes broke her heart. The last thing she wanted to do was hurt him. If he needed affection to feel better about their relationship, then she was going to have to muster up the necessary emotions. The fact that she had not taken Xanax in two days would make it easier. "Let's go upstairs," she said quietly to him. "Our friends won't miss us."

Jason raised his eyebrows. "Really?"

Cathy nodded. "I love you, and I'm not trying to be cold toward you. I just haven't felt much of anything lately."

Jason took her hand and led her out of the kitchen and up to his bedroom. He locked the door behind him after they entered the room. Without hesitance, he lifted her off the ground and playfully tossed her down on his bed. She laughed as she thought of the first night they met. While laughing, she saw the sparkle return to Jason's eyes.

Jason climbed on top of her and began to kiss her lips, then her cheek, then her neck, and then behind her ear. As he did, she began to feel more emotion than she had felt in weeks. She kissed him back and unbuttoned his shirt before pulling it off him. In return, he began unbuttoning her shirt and kissing her body as each new piece of skin was revealed. A surge of pleasure shot through her veins, and she was relieved to realize that she still wanted him. Pulling his body close to hers, she rubbed his back as he continued to kiss her.

At that point, Cathy was glad she had not taken Xanax because everything she was feeling was wonderful. She had forgotten that Jason's touch brought her joy. They had hardly hooked up over the last few months because she had no drive to do so. She was thankful that Jason had not put any pressure on her to be physical, but she felt bad about neglecting him. "I'm sorry," she said quietly. "We should have been doing this all summer."

"It's okay," Jason replied and ran his hand through her wavy hair before rolling onto his side to lie beside her. She rolled onto her side to face him while he reached for her hand. "I'm just happy you seem into me."

"I am into you," Cathy stated earnestly. "Right now, I feel everything I used to feel when we first started hooking up."

"Good."

Cathy embraced him as she felt tears glaze her eyes. "Jay," she said softly, "why don't we get more naked and cuddle?"

"More naked?" he asked and pulled away from her to look into her eyes. "As in, like, I take off my pants or you take off your skirt?"

Cathy smiled. "As in, let's both get completely naked."

Jason widened his eyes. "That's a huge step."

"I know," Cathy said, "but I feel bad that I've been so distant lately."

"Don't worry about it," Jason assured her. "You don't have to prove anything to me. I know it was just the pills affecting your emotions. Don't feel pressured to do anything with me that you haven't done before."

"I don't," Cathy responded. "I just want to feel closer to you."

Jason searched her eyes, looking as though he was contemplating something. "I don't think I'm ready to be naked with you," he admitted a few seconds later.

"Why not?" Cathy asked and peered at him in confusion.

Jason sighed. "Because it will be really hard for me not to try to have sex with you," he replied. "I want you more than I've ever wanted anything. Seeing you naked would be torture."

"Well, what if only *you* got naked?"

Jason laughed. "I'm fine with that."

Cathy smiled and rolled on top of him. She unbuttoned his jeans and pulled them down to his ankles. Then, she slowly pulled his boxer shorts down, inch by inch, kissing him every step of the way. Her eyes widened, and her stomach fluttered when she saw her boyfriend's private parts for the first time. Jason began to laugh at her expression and rolled over so that he could lie on top of her.

"Maybe you could take off my skirt and just leave on my underwear," she suggested.

"That's risky," Jason warned her. "I don't think I need to be turned on more than I already am," he added.

"I'm sorry," she said. "I'm not trying to tease you."

"Then keep your skirt on," Jason stated emphatically.

"Okay," she agreed. "Just cuddle with me. I don't care if we miss the party."

Jason let out a sigh of relief. "This is the first time I've felt like I've had you back in months," he said as he rolled onto his side so that he could be the big spoon. He wrapped his arms around her tightly and pulled her body close to his.

"It's the first time I've felt like myself in a while," she admitted and squeezed his hands.

"I'll lie here with you all night if you want," Jason offered. "Our friends won't miss us," he added.

"I'm glad Leslie and Alyssa are here with Lisa," Cathy stated. "She's nervous about seeing Chris."

"He's nervous, too."

"So, he's really been staying away from pills?"

"Yeah, he's doing well."

"I'm sure Lisa will be happy to hear he's still clean of the bad stuff. It's been a few months now."

"I know you don't like her, but I think Courtney is helping him a lot."

"It's not that I don't like her," Cathy admitted; "I just don't like what she and Chris are doing to Bryan."

"I'm glad we're not downstairs," Jason admitted. "Bryan is probably here by now, and he hasn't seen Chris since he found out about Courtney. It's going to be awkward. Bryan says he's not mad at him, but Chris feels bad. I think he's kind of dating her now."

"Really? I thought they were just friends."

"They were, but I think it's become more than that."

"Did they hook up?"

"They kissed the other day," Jason replied. "I haven't heard anything more than that."

"Wow. She made Bryan wait an awfully long time to kiss her. She's only known Chris for, like, a month!" Cathy exclaimed.

"I know. I feel bad."

"So, they're together now? Geez. Lisa isn't going to be happy about that."

"Lisa and Chris are no good for each other," Jason stated matter-of-factly. "They're both broken. They need partners like Jeff and Courtney to stabilize them."

"Lisa's acting strange. She told me she smoked a cigarette the other day."

"Oh, at my house? Yeah, I saw that. You were in the pool."

"No, with Alyssa and Leslie."

"I wouldn't worry about it. Knowing Lisa, she had an ulterior motive. Jeff made an offhanded comment, saying he would smoke weed the day he saw her smoke a cigarette. She wants him to try weed, so she's probably trying to hold him to what he said."

"Why did Jeff say that? He doesn't smoke, and he hates drugs."

"He wanted her to stop asking him to try weed. He assumed she would never smoke a cigarette."

"I never thought Lisa, Leslie, or Alyssa would. Jon would probably break up with Alyssa if he found out she tried it," Cathy speculated. "I think he still loves Chantal anyway."

"Definitely," Jason agreed, "and that's why it's good Chantal has nothing to do with him. Andy's way better for her—even if he and his friends think we are awful people."

"Aside from Leslie and Jeff, their whole preppy clique is stuck up," Cathy said. "I actually think Lisa's a bit of snob, too."

"She's a brat," Jason said with a laugh. "I've been telling you that forever."

***

Nearly two hours later, Cathy and Jason were still cuddling in his bed when they heard three loud knocks on his door, followed by Chris's deep voice saying, "Jay! The cops are here!"

Jason shot his blue eyes open and quickly jumped out of bed. Cathy watched him frantically begin putting on his clothes. She hopped out of bed and grabbed her shirt off the floor. She was still buttoning it when he opened the door to reveal Chris, Jon, Bryan, and Alyssa. "Go up to my parents' room!" Jason ordered them, motioning for his friends to run down the hallway to his left. "Cathy, c'mon!"

"I'm coming!" she cried, rushing toward the door while buttoning her last few buttons. She followed the group down the hallway and up a set of stairs that led to Jason's parents' suite.

After they entered the bedroom, Jason locked the door behind them without turning on any lights. "Go through the bathroom and into the dressing room," he directed. "I'll lock the doors behind us." After everyone was in the windowless dressing room, Jason turned on the light, illuminating shelves of clothing, pocketbooks, and shoes. Cathy sat down on a stool and anxiously peered at her friends. She could not help but wonder if they had seen her buttoning her shirt and if any of them thought she and Jason had sex.

"Where are Lisa and Leslie?" Jason asked, glancing curiously from Chris to Alyssa.

"We couldn't find them before we ran upstairs," Alyssa replied.

"They weren't in the kitchen when we heard the cops knock on the door," Chris said. "We only had enough time to run up the back stairs."

"They're supposed to sleep over my house tonight, so I know they didn't leave," Cathy gathered.

"They're both pretty smart. I'm sure they found a good hiding spot," Chris remarked. "Oh, I grabbed the cookies off the counter so no cops would see them," he added and held up a large plastic bag. "Do you want one, Cathy?"

Cathy shook her head. "It's too late. I have to be home by eleven. I can't go home high. How wild was it downstairs?"

"It was mainly Matt's friends, so it wasn't rowdy," Chris replied. "The cops know Matt is the captain of the football team. They'll cut him some slack. They always cut Taylor and Jordan slack."

"Let's hope," Jason muttered. "Our summer fun will be cut short if my parents find out about this."

"Hopefully the cops will be gone by the time your mom comes," Alyssa said and glanced at Cathy.

"They will be," Jason asserted. "It's not like Matt's friends have drugs on them."

"What if they search your house and find Luke's stash?" Cathy asked, widening her eyes.

Jason gasped. "Oh, dear God. It better be locked up and out of sight."

Cathy thought her boyfriend looked nervous, which was a peculiar sight. Neither Chris nor Jon appeared worried, and Bryan's expression was as hard to read as usual. He was standing opposite Chris, and Cathy wondered if he knew about Chris and Courtney's kiss.

***

A half hour later, Jason crept through his parents' bedroom to look out the window. He saw no sign of flashing-blue lights or cruisers in his driveway. "You guys stay in there," Jason called to his friends. "I'm going to scope out the scene downstairs."

As he walked out of his parents' bedroom and down to the second floor, he prayed that his brothers were not in trouble. As he neared the back staircase that led to the kitchen, he heard familiar voices and let out a sigh of relief. The chatter sounded light, so the cops must have left quickly. When Jason entered his large kitchen, he saw his brothers, Marc, Michelle, Katie, Ally, Lisa, Leslie, and about a dozen other kids in Matt's grade.

"Look who decided to join the party," Lisa taunted him as he walked over to her.

He rolled his eyes. "Where did you hide?" he asked.

"In the closet underneath your stairs," Lisa replied. "It's basically a secret passageway."

"Smart. What did the cops do?" Jason asked, glancing from Lisa to Leslie.

"It sounded like they just walked around the kitchen and scoped out the scene," Leslie replied. "Someone hid the keg, so they never saw it."

"When they saw 'good kids' like Marc Dunkin and Michelle Taylor, they realized it wasn't a wild party," Lisa said. "They left within five minutes."

"Good. How have things been between you and Chris tonight?" Jason asked curiously.

Lisa shrugged. "We didn't really talk. He was mainly talking with the older kids—probably to avoid me and Bryan."

Jason cocked his head to the side. "Why would he avoid Bryan?" he questioned her, playing dumb.

Lisa smirked. "Her initials are CA."

Jason widened his eyes. "Did Cathy tell you?!"

Lisa laughed. "No, but you just did. I had my suspicions. The tension between Chris and Bryan was perceivable. Courtney broke up with him right after meeting you guys. It sounds to me like she wants Chris."

"They're just hanging out," Jason stated, wondering if Lisa was jealous. "She's straightedge and a good influence on him."

"Well, that's probably what he needs," Lisa said with a careless shrug.

Jason lowered his eyebrows and peered at her. As nonchalant as she sounded, he perceived sadness in her eyes. "Why didn't Jeff come?" he asked.

"He didn't want to make it awkward for me or Chris," Lisa replied.

"Are you two a couple yet?" Jason questioned her.

"Something like that," Lisa replied and smiled slightly.

"Good," Jason stated flatly. "I like him."

"Jeff's great," Lisa remarked and met Jason's eyes. "Maybe I'll bring him to your next party."

"You should," Jason said before leaving the kitchen to fetch everyone else. It was clear that Lisa still had feelings for Chris. As convenient as it had been for two of his closest friends to date, Jason knew that Lisa and Chris brought out the worst in each other. With that thought, he began to wonder if he brought out the worst in Cathy.

CHAPTER 6

As the summer progressed, Cathy replaced Xanax with edibles at Jason's request. This, however, made her care more about *everything* than she had during the previous months, including Jason's use of alcohol. She thought it made him more outspoken and brought out his propensity to tease others, which everyone found humorous except for Cathy.

Jason, of course, was thankful that Cathy had laid her Xanax infatuation to rest. He had not quite weaned himself off Adderall, but he had restrained himself from snorting it. With school starting, he did not want to risk losing his focus, but soon he planned to decipher if weed and Adderall were merely cancelling each other out.

Throughout August, numerous parties took place: one at Lisa's, a few at "the pit" in the woods behind the high school, and a couple at Chris's house. At one of Chris's parties, Jason was able to convince Cathy to drink.

"Be my beer pong partner," he pleaded with her. "You won't get drunk off the small amount of beer in the cups."

Cathy sighed. "Don't pressure me."

"You told me getting drunk is a sin, not drinking," Jason retorted.

Cathy rolled her eyes. "I can be your partner without drinking."

"Then that means I'll have to drink every cup."

Cathy widened her eyes. "I don't want that to happen!"

Knowing that she hated when he got drunk, Jason smiled. "So, be my partner and have a few sips of beer. You won't get drunk. I promise."

"Fine," Cathy acquiesced.

She and Jason ended up winning multiple rounds and playing at the table longer than anticipated. When they finally lost a game, Jason could tell Cathy was slightly buzzed, but he did not think she seemed drunk by any means.

"Let's go upstairs," she whispered after affectionately throwing her arms around him.

Jason widened his eyes excitedly. "Okay," he said and took her hand. "Hopefully one of the guest rooms is free." He led her into the room in which they had watched *Friday Night Lights* on the night they met. After gently tossing her down onto the king-sized bed, he climbed on top of her.

She pulled his t-shirt over his head and threw it to the ground. Then, she pushed him over so that she was on top of him. "I want to see you naked again," she said.

Jason laughed. "It's my lucky day."

She pulled his shorts and boxers off of him without any hesitation and then smiled. "You have such a good body!" she cried. "I'm so lucky. You're the best-looking guy I know."

"Thanks, babe," Jason said with a wide grin. "You're pretty hot, yourself. Although, I've never seen you naked."

"Do you want to?" Cathy asked and raised her eyebrows.

Jason laughed. "Of course I do, but it's not a good idea."

"Oh, I think it's a *great* idea," Cathy said and pulled her shirt over her head.

Jason lowered his eyebrows and wondered what had gotten into his girlfriend. *A little bit of beer shouldn't make her this horny. Maybe it's just time?* he thought. *We have been together for over a year.* He rolled Cathy over so that he was on top of her. "Are you sure you want to get naked?" he asked. "You know what could happen, right?"

Cathy nodded. "I want to know you the way other girls have known you."

Jason laughed. "You know me better than anyone does."

"You know what I mean."

Jason gazed at her thoughtfully, confused by her sudden interest in sex. "Are you sure?" he asked hesitantly.

Cathy nodded.

"Okay, then hold on," he said and hopped off her. He reached into his shorts' pocket and pulled a condom out of his wallet. A few seconds later, he climbed back on top of Cathy and began removing the rest of her clothes. "I love you," he said and looked directly into her green eyes.

"I love you too," she replied and smiled.

***

Around nine o'clock the following morning, Cathy woke up in Chris's spare bedroom. Jason's arms were wrapped tightly around her, and she felt panicked. She had planned to sleep at Alyssa's the night before. "Crap!" she said out loud as she sat up straight. "Ouch!" she cried as she felt an unfamiliar pain in her private area.

She stood up and began gathering her clothes on the ground. As she did, she realized the pain felt worse with movement. When she went to grab her skirt, she noticed a dirty condom on the floor beside it. She felt the color drain from her face as she dropped her jaw and darted her eyes at Jason. Her heart began pounding in her chest, and nausea overtook her. "Oh, my, God," she said loudly and then covered her mouth. She began shaking at the realization she had likely lost her virginity.

Jason opened his eyes and peered at her. "What's wrong?" he asked with a concerned expression.

"Did we have sex last night?" she asked, sure that she looked horrified.

Jason sat up and cocked his head to the side. "You don't remember?"

Cathy shook her head as tears filled her eyes.

Jason's facial expression fell. "Why don't you remember?"

Cathy blinked and stared at him speechlessly.

"Why don't you remember?" he repeated before climbing out of bed and kneeling beside her.

Cathy swallowed the large lump in her throat. "I drank last night, didn't I?" she questioned him.

"You weren't drunk," Jason replied. "I never would have touched you if you were."

Cathy dropped her eyes to the floor.

"Why don't you remember what happened?" he pressed.

"Am I sore because we went to third base? Or did we have sex?" she asked and looked up at her boyfriend, who appeared extremely disturbed.

"Cathy, is this some type of joke?" he questioned her. "We had sex, and you weren't drunk."

Tears began to plunge from her eyes. "What have I done?!" she cried. "I am a horrible person."

Jason threw his arms around her. "You are not a horrible person. We love each other, and we've been dating for well over a year. You need to tell me *right now* why you don't remember last night."

Cathy sobbed in his arms. "I took Xanax before the party," she admitted after a few seconds of hesitation. "I didn't want you to know."

Jason released her from his embrace.

Cathy glanced up at him. He looked as though he were at a loss for words. "I'm sorry," she added and touched his face. "I wanted our first time to be special, and I ruined it. I don't even remember what you feel like inside me."

Jason remained speechless, and Cathy assumed he felt as though he had somehow taken advantage of her. That was clearly not the case, and as upset as she was, she knew she had to make him feel better about the situation. "I've wanted to have sex with you for a while," she assured him. "I guess the alcohol gave me the confidence I needed to express that."

Jason raised his eyebrows and eyed her warily.

"You didn't do anything wrong," she added.

"Then why are you crying?" Jason questioned her.

Because I lost my virginity and wanted to get married a virgin, she thought. "Because I'll never remember our first time," she replied. She couldn't stand to see him look upset. Jason had never once been forceful with her, so she assumed she had come onto him.

"Why did you take Xanax?" Jason asked. "Did you run out of gummy worms?"

Cathy shook her head. "No. I just wanted to socialize and have fun last night. The gummies keep my anxiety at bay, but they make me quiet. Xanax helps me be social."

Jason let out a heavy breath. "Please flush all the Xanax you have left down the toilet. Can't you see the damage it causes? You'll never remember one of the most special nights of your life."

Cathy dropped her eyes to the floor. "I shouldn't have touched alcohol."

"Obviously," Jason stated emphatically. "You know what drinking on Xanax did to Chris. Why didn't you just say no?"

"Because I didn't want you to know that I took Xanax," Cathy replied. "I didn't want you to worry about me."

"Well, now I feel like a rapist!" Jason exclaimed.

Cathy looked up at him. "You are not a rapist," she said and placed her hand on his shoulder. She lowered her eyebrows in concern. "You are the love of my life and the boy I have wanted to lose my virginity to for over a year."

"But not like this," Jason commented and shook his head. "Last night was so special to me, but now it means less because you don't remember it. Xanax tainted such a special memory."

"I'm sorry," Cathy said and looked down at her fingernails. "Next time, I'll be completely sober."

"If there is a next time," Jason muttered.

Cathy darted her eyes at him, questioningly.

"What? Can you blame me for thinking you didn't want to sleep with me?" he asked. "I woke up to you crying on the floor."

Cathy closed her eyes and took a deep breath. She opened her eyes and gazed lovingly at her boyfriend. "How can I fix this?"

Jason sighed. "Don't take Xanax ever again. See if alcohol relaxes you. It typically makes people more social. You can get buzzed without getting drunk."

"Okay," Cathy agreed.

"But don't eat a gummy on nights you're going to drink," Jason added. "You'll get too messed up."

"Okay," Cathy said and then wiped tears from her eyes. "My mom is supposed to pick me up at Alyssa's at eleven. I don't know what to do."

"Why don't we walk to the coffee shop and buy a bunch of pastries?" Jason suggested. "We can show up at her house with breakfast so her family won't think it's weird you're coming over so early. I'm sure Alyssa and Lisa came up with some excuse for your absence last night. Maybe you could call your mom and ask if you can spend the day there. I'd like to hang out with you today if you're up for it."

"Good idea, per usual," Cathy commented and slowly stood up. She hated the feeling between her legs. "My mom is going to wonder why I'm limping."

"She's not going to think we had sex," Jason asserted and stood up beside her. "You just turned fifteen. I bet she thinks we're way too young for sex."

"Weren't you twelve when you lost your virginity?" Cathy questioned him.

Jason nodded. "Yeah, but I turned thirteen a few weeks later."

Cathy rolled her eyes. "I'm not even going to tell Lisa about this. Please don't tell anyone."

"You have nothing to worry about," he said and wrapped his arm around her shoulders. "Let's go get breakfast."

CHAPTER 7

IT TOOK TWO WEEKS for Cathy to feel ready to sleep with Jason again. This time she was completely sober. Although she felt guilty about having pre-marital sex, she wanted to do it one more time so she could remember it. She reasoned that they could stop sleeping together afterward, and she assumed Jason would be okay with that. Therefore, one August afternoon she invited him to her house while her parents were at work, her little sister Stephanie was at camp, and Chantal was out with Andy.

She played one of the most romantic songs she had ever heard—"Crash Into Me" by Dave Matthews Band—as she prepared herself for what was about to happen. Jason made sure there was plenty of foreplay so sex would not hurt Cathy as much as it had the first time. However, when he went inside her, she felt more pain than she had anticipated. "Ouch," she winced. "Go really slow."

"Of course," Jason said and kissed her forehead. "It will hurt a lot less the more we do it."

Cathy swallowed a large lump in her throat. She was afraid to mention that she wanted this to be their last time. It was not because of the discomfort but rather because of her religious beliefs. The idea of acting sinfully by continually fornicating made her queasy. She knew enough scripture to realize that once people slept together, they were bound in a spiritual way. In Biblical times, Jewish men were commanded to marry the girls they slept with in order not to "shame" them. However, she could not imagine herself getting married until after college. *How are we going to wait eight years to have sex again?* When Jason climbed off her, Cathy felt sore.

"Now, that was special," Jason commented as he lay beside her in bed. "It actually felt to me like it was your first time."

"Well, that makes two of us," Cathy remarked dryly.

Jason turned onto his side and gently touched her face. "I love you," he said and gazed into her eyes.

She smiled at him. "I love you, too."

"What time do your parents usually get home from work?" he asked.

"Six, so we have some time," Cathy replied.

Jason raised his eyebrows. "Do you think we can do it again in a little bit? Or are you too sore?"

Cathy widened her eyes, realizing how horny her boyfriend truly was. "I think I'm a little too sore," she replied, hoping he would wait a while before asking again.

"That's okay," he said. "You can't blame me for trying, though," he added with a laugh. "Roll over. I'll be the big spoon."

As Jason wrapped her tightly in her arms, she felt safe. She hoped sex would not change their relationship. Despite the comfort of being in his arms, she began to wonder if he would lose interest in her now that he'd had her physically. After all, the other girls he slept with had not kept his interest for very long. She feared she could be added to that list. It was at that moment when her anxiety kicked in, her palms began to sweat, and her heart began to pound.

"I think I'm about to have an anxiety attack," she said and pulled free from his grip. "I need to use the bathroom. I'll be right back."

Jason was wearing a concerned expression when Cathy climbed out of bed. When she returned a few minutes later, he still appeared worried. "Are you okay?" he asked.

Cathy nodded. "I just washed my face and my hands with warm water," she replied. "It calmed me down."

"Did you take Xanax?"

Cathy shook her head. "No. I want to stay completely sober today. I don't want to forget anything."

Jason smiled. "Come back in bed and cuddle with me. I could use a nap."

Cathy walked over to her nightstand and set an alarm for 5:45 p.m. "We just have to be downstairs before my parents get home," she said and climbed into bed beside him. He, again, wrapped her in his arms, and they slept until her alarm went off.

CHAPTER 8

***

DURING THE LAST WEEK of summer, Jason could not contain how excited he was to soon attend the same school as his best friends. He had been trying all week to convince Chris to throw a party the night before school started. Chris, who had been spending most of his time with Courtney, had refrained from using any drugs beyond weed or alcohol for over a month.

"We've been dreaming of this day for years," Jason said to Chris over the phone one late-August evening. "I'd like to start the morning with all of our crew under one roof."

"Well, my parents are leaving me in charge of the house this time, so we could make it happen," Chris said in an uneasy tone, "but no one's parents are going to let them stay out late on a school night."

"What if the party started in the middle of the night?" Jason proposed. "I can easily sneak out of my house. I'm sure most of our friends can."

"What are you going to do? Walk?" Chris asked. Jason's home was in the prestigious Hamilton section of Montgomery—far from Chris's house, which was near the lake.

"Luke can drive," Jason assumed. "My parents will be sound asleep, and as long as he doesn't park in the garage, they won't hear his car leave the driveway. BMWs are basically silent. We can pick up Cathy and anyone else on the way."

"I'm probably going to regret agreeing to this," Chris said reluctantly.

"No, you won't," Jason sang. "You'll love every second of it. I'll come over as early as I can. My parents usually go to bed around nine."

Chris sighed. "Fine. Spread the word," he acquiesced.

***

On the last day of summer break, Jason convinced his parents to let him spend the day at Chris's house. Luke offered to "pick Jason up at nine" so his parents could go to bed. Since Jason and Luke had never given their parents a reason not to trust them, it never crossed Mr. or Mrs. Davids' mind that the boys would stay out later than what had been agreed upon.

Spending the day together gave Jason and Chris plenty of time to pre-game before the other guests arrived. After a couple of hours of drinking and watching the Red Sox game, Jason grew bored... bored enough to want to trip. "If we do it before the party, it will wear off way before we go to school," Jason reasoned, trying to persuade Chris. "I know you've been staying away from drugs, but this is a special occasion."

"Isn't Cathy coming?" Chris asked. "Won't she get pissed if you're on acid?"

Jason shrugged. "If she shows up completely sober, it'll be a problem."

Chris cocked his head to the side. "Now that she's off Xanax, has she been giving you a hard time about anything?"

Jason shook his head. "She's been fine lately. Adderall doesn't bother her, as long as I don't snort it. I'm just glad she stopped taking Xanax."

"She's still cold toward me," Chris remarked.

"She's just upset about you and Courtney because of Bryan and Lisa."

"People move on," Chris stated matter-of-factly.

"Have you actually moved on?"

Chris shrugged. "I'm trying my best, but honestly, I'm less attracted to Courtney than I used to be. Don't take this the wrong way, but I think Cathy has rubbed off on her."

"How is that even possible? Cathy barely knows her."

"Court wants to become friends with her so badly. She started wearing makeup and dressing up on a daily basis. I think she's trying to look like the other girls we hang out with. She's never met Alyssa or Lisa, but she's seen plenty of pictures of them online. She knows we hang out with the prettiest girls in our grade."

"I'd put Katherine Rossi on that list too—even though she won't hang out with us anymore," Jason commented.

"Definitely," Chris agreed. "But my point is that I think Courtney saw how pretty Lisa is and started to feel threatened. I know I'm partial, but I think Lisa's the hottest girl I've ever met. I'm sure you feel the same way about Cathy."

"Yeah, and Bryan feels that way about Courtney," Jason interjected and raised his eyebrows. "I can't believe he doesn't hate you, guy."

"That's a whole different story," Chris said, "which I don't want to talk about. If he comes tonight, he'll ignore me, but he'll notice the change in Court. I think she's becoming shallow. She's kind of been acting like Alyssa."

Jason let out a short laugh. "Alyssa? Anyone shallow enough to date their best friend's ex is… oh… wait… that would be you, too. Never mind."

"Eff you!" Chris exclaimed.

"You walked into that one. Alyssa's no shallower than you, buddy."

Chris laughed. "Fine. Point taken. Alyssa and I are both selfish and shallow."

Jason shook his head. "You guys are fine."

"Court wants to fit in," Chris assumed. "I get it, but she's more attractive when she wears no makeup and acts like herself."

"I haven't seen her recently, but I can't imagine her acting anything like Alyssa." Jason did not mean that in a bad way; he adored Alyssa. In fact, she had been the first girl accepted into their group of friends. She was the one who brought Lisa and Leslie into their clique. She befriended Chantal and eventually Cathy. What Jason meant was he could not picture someone as down-to-earth as Courtney acting like the most fashion-savvy, image-conscious girl in their social circle.

"Talk to her tonight," Chris said. "You'll see what I mean."

"So, she's really coming?"

Chris nodded. "She said she's coming with Luke. He offered to pick her up before he gets Cathy. She lives near you."

"Oh, God. Hopefully he doesn't offer her drugs," Jason said and widened his eyes. "Luke could easily horrify your girlfriend."

"He knows better than to do that," Chris stated. "He's friends with her sister, who used to have a drug problem. Plus, he told me he's only planning to drink tonight."

"Who bought alcohol for him?"

"He said Taylor bought him some beer balls for the weekend, so he's going to bring a couple over," Chris replied.

"Oh, yeah, my parents are going away Friday night," Jason recalled. "Luke must be planning a party."

"That's what he told T the beer was for. T would never have bought for Luke if he knew some of it was for my house."

"Why is my brother in touch with your cousin?" Jason asked.

Chris shrugged. "He probably called him because he needed someone twenty-one to buy the alcohol. I doubt any of Luke's friends' fake IDs are good enough for buying a beer ball."

"That makes sense. How is Taylor? Is he going to play this year?"

Chris let out a short laugh. "No. I don't even want to get into his story right now. He's nowhere near ready to get back on the field."

"His knee must be healed by now. No?"

"He's not in the right mind," Chris said and shook his head. "I can't get into it. Marc asked me not to talk about it with anyone."

"No worries," Jason said, wondering what was wrong with Taylor. "But if we're going to trip, we should take it soon. Are you sure you want to do it with Courtney coming here?"

"I'm not sure I want to do it at all," Chris replied. "This is the first time I've drank in a week. I've been doing really well."

"Once you're drunk, you'll want to trip," Jason reasoned. "It's inevitable."

Chris sighed. "That's probably true. If I take it now, I'll be fine when Courtney gets here," he pondered. "If I wait 'til I'm drunk, I won't be. I have the same tabs from last month. They only lasted eight or nine hours. It's four now, so when Court gets here, I wouldn't be peaking."

"So, we should take it now," Jason proposed. "My night will be better if Cathy can't tell I'm tripping."

"She'll be able to tell," Chris assured him. "You get weird, dude. She hates when you trip, and she thinks you've only eaten mushrooms."

Jason sighed. "Hopefully, Luke gives her some alcohol on the ride over to loosen her up."

"I'm just happy you'll drink with me again," Chris said. "It had been a ridiculously long time since we broke into my dad's liquor cabinet."

Jason laughed, recalling an incident from two years prior. "Well, I got *ridiculously* sick. My parents made me get tested for mono because I was in bed for two days. To this day, I gag if I smell gin. I thought for the longest time that I would never drink again."

"You're the idiot who drank the rest of the bottle," Chris said with a short laugh.

Jason nodded. "I learned a lot about pacing myself that night, and that's part of the reason why I want to trip. I'm already buzzed, and if I keep drinking, I'm going to get sick."

Chris sighed. "Fine. We can drop acid, but let's do it now so we're not wrecked when everyone else gets here."

CHAPTER 9

AT ELEVEN-THIRTY THAT EVENING, Cathy crept through the darkness of her home. Her best route of escape would be through the slider in her basement because it silently slid shut. After leaving her house, she walked across her yard and up her street to the intersection with Pico Ave.—her planned meeting spot with Luke. Within a few minutes, he pulled up in his new BMW. His girlfriend Missy was riding shotgun, and Courtney was sitting behind her. "Hop in the back," Luke called after rolling down the passenger-side window.

Cathy walked around the car so she could sit behind Luke. After closing the door, she glanced at Courtney, who greeted her with a friendly smile. Cathy was surprised to see Courtney dressed up in a skirt, blouse, and high heels. She was wearing eyeliner, mascara, and lip gloss, which made her look much older than fourteen. Cathy wondered if Chris had asked Courtney to dress up or if Courtney was trying to look more like Cathy and her friends.

"CK, I have a present for you in that red bag on the floor," Luke said as soon as he began driving.

Cathy widened her eyes. "I can only imagine what it is," she muttered, hoping he was not going to tempt her with Xanax.

"You'll be happy," Luke assured her.

Cathy picked the insulated bag up off the floor and put it in her lap. After unzipping it, she saw a bunch of little nips—all different flavors of Doctor McGillicuddy's, including peppermint, grape, root beer, apple pie, and butterscotch. "Where did you get these?" she asked as she selected a peppermint one.

"A friend," Luke responded. "Drink as many as you want. Jay has been pre-gaming with Chris all day. If you don't show up with a buzz, he's going to annoy you to no end."

Cathy laughed. "Thanks," she said and took a butterscotch one out the bag before zipping it shut. "Oh, Courtney, do you want one?" she asked and glanced at her.

Courtney shook her head and dropped her blue eyes to the floor. "No, thanks."

Cathy smiled and put the bag back on the ground. She finished both shots before they were halfway to Chris's house, so she decided to have another.

"Pass an apple pie and a grape one up here," Luke said after hearing her unzip the bag.

Cathy handed the shots to Missy and watched as Missy handed the apple pie one to Luke with its cap off. "Cheers," Luke sang before throwing back the miniature bottle. Missy drank the grape one while Cathy downed a root beer one—which was way too sweet for her taste buds.

Cathy glanced at Courtney and thought she looked horrified. Knowing Chris's house was only five minutes away, Cathy was not worried about Luke being too drunk to drive. She doubted five of those shots would have impaired his judgment. As against alcohol as she had once been, Cathy was starting to believe it was better for social situations than the drugs she had been trying. Xanax had too many risks associated with it, and a half of a milligram was no longer sufficient to relax her; edibles kept her anxiety at bay but made her antisocial; alcohol, on the other hand, cheered her up and made her more outgoing. Although she believed getting drunk was not only sinful, but also foolish, she thought getting buzzed was harmless. Learning her limit would be key, and if she was going to continue to drink at social events, she would need to figure it out sooner rather than later.

The next time Cathy glanced at Courtney, she thought she looked incredibly uncomfortable. "You look really pretty," Cathy complimented her, hoping to help Courtney relax. "I like your shirt."

Courtney smiled. "Thanks. You do, too."

Cathy looked down at the yellow dress and sandals she was wearing. "My best friend helped me pick out this dress. I'm not very fashion savvy without her help."

"Alyssa or Lisa?" Courtney asked.

"Lisa," Cathy replied.

"Is she going to be at Chris's tonight?" Courtney inquired.

Cathy nodded. "If she can sneak out of her house without her brothers catching her, she'll be there."

Courtney cringed. "I'm nervous about meeting her," she admitted. "I'm sure she's nice, but I'm afraid she won't like me because I'm going out with Chris."

"Lisa's great, but I would keep your distance," Cathy cautioned her. "She has a new boyfriend, but she and Chris have two years' worth of history. It will be best if you don't interact with her at all."

Courtney nodded. "Thanks for the advice."

"You'll get along fine with Alyssa if she's there," Cathy added. "She's super friendly and easy to talk to."

"I'm looking forward to meeting her," Courtney said. "I really like Jon, so I'm sure I'll like her."

Cathy did not want to like Courtney because she hated that she had hurt Bryan, but at the same time, she knew how awkward it was to be the new person in a clique. She recognized the discomfort in Courtney's tone and body language. This pulled on Cathy's heartstrings and made her want to comfort her. Clearly without Xanax, Cathy's empathy was back in full swing.

When they arrived at Chris's house, they found the living room and kitchen filled with Montgomery Lake High teenagers. Luke and Missy took off immediately to bring the beer balls to the bar in the basement while Cathy and Courtney searched for their boyfriends.

"Hey, Jon," Cathy greeted him halfheartedly. "Have you seen Jay or Chris anywhere?"

"Oh, hey, girls," Jon said and turned around to hug Courtney. Thankfully, he spared Cathy from an embrace she didn't want. "I think Jay is upstairs. I haven't seen Chris in a while."

"Okay, thanks," Cathy said. "Let's go upstairs and see if we can find them," she suggested. She could not fathom why her boyfriend wasn't smack dab in the middle of the festivities.

Leading Courtney up Chris's grand bridal staircase, Cathy felt her heart begin to pound. She hoped she would not find Jason passed out or puking. The last thing he needed was to be sick on the first day of high school. Cathy let out a sigh of relief when she noticed him sitting in the study a moment later. "Hey!" she exclaimed happily.

Jason looked up from the book he was holding. "Hi!" he cried and smiled widely.

"What are you doing?" Cathy asked with a short laugh while making her way over to hug him.

He hugged her back tightly and ran his hand through her hair. "Your hair feels so soft."

Cathy pulled away from him and looked into his eyes. His pupils were dilated—more dilated than they typically got from edibles. "Why are you upstairs by yourself?" she asked as she peered at him suspiciously.

"I just needed to get away from the crowd and think," Jason replied nonchalantly. "Hi, Courtney."

"Hi," Courtney said quietly with a perplexed expression on her face.

"What were you thinking about?" Cathy asked curiously.

Jason let out a nervous-sounding laugh. "Oh, you know, just about how time is relative and not actually real," he replied.

Cathy let out a heavy breath. "Keep thinking about that while I help Courtney find Chris," she said and turned abruptly away from her boyfriend. "Let's go downstairs, Court."

Courtney followed Cathy without hesitation out of the room and down the stairs. She looked incredibly baffled by Jason's behavior.

Passing by Luke, Cathy asked, "Have you seen Chris, anywhere?"

"No," Luke replied, "but some people are out on the deck."

"Okay. Thanks," Cathy said and took Courtney's hand to pull her through the crowded kitchen. When she opened the door that led outside, her eyes immediately met with Bryan's. "Hey!" she greeted him warmly as he stepped past her into the house.

"Hi!" he responded in a surprised tone and then quickly darted his brown eyes at Courtney. He pushed past them without another word, and Cathy felt overwhelmed with emotion. She feared Bryan would think she had betrayed him by showing up with Courtney.

As she stepped onto the deck, she spotted Chris across the way, standing with Lisa and smoking a cigarette. Her heart began to pound as she realized how awkward things were about to become.

"Hey! I thought you quit smoking?!" Courtney suddenly exclaimed and pushed past Cathy towards Chris.

"Court!" Chris cried and whipped around to see her. He threw his cigarette to the ground and stomped on it. "I'm sorry. I'm a little drunk."

"You stink!" she complained after throwing her arms around him.

Chris laughed. "I'll go wash my hands and brush my teeth. I'm sorry. Let's go inside," he said and pulled Courtney toward his house. "What's up, Cathy?" he greeted her in passing.

"Hey," Cathy said and gazed into his eyes to see if his pupils were dilated. It was too dark outside for her to tell. After Chris and Courtney walked inside the house, Cathy stayed outside with Lisa. "So, you guys talked?" she gathered.

Lisa nodded. "He smoked in front of me. Do you think that means he's over me?" she asked, sounding a bit paranoid.

"I think he's probably just drunk," Cathy replied, "or maybe he heard that you tried smoking and didn't think it would bother you."

Lisa looked distraught. "He tossed it down the second he saw Courtney. What if he's in love with her?"

"Are you in love with Jeff?" Cathy questioned her rhetorically. "People rebound. It's human nature. Chris is rebounding."

"I hope so," Lisa said downheartedly.

"What were you guys talking about?"

"Oh, he was telling me all sorts of stuff," Lisa replied and widened her green eyes: "how he's been clean of benzos and opiates since our breakup; how MLH wants him on the JV football team; how he only drank once this week; and how he hasn't rolled or taken Adderall in months."

"Well, that's good. It sounds like he wants you to know he's on a better path."

"Yeah, but he was way more expressive than usual," Lisa stated. "It only took me a few minutes to realize he was tripping. He kept touching my shoulder and commenting on how soft my shirt felt. He said my eyes looked greener than ever. His senses were hyperaware."

"At least Chris is social when he trips!" Cathy exclaimed. "Jason turns into a weirdo. He gets so in his head that he only wants to sit around and think. I just found him alone in the study. He told me he was thinking about how time isn't real."

Lisa laughed. "Do mushrooms and acid affect him the same way?"

"Acid?" Cathy asked, caught off guard by the question. "He's never tripped on acid."

Lisa eyed Cathy in an amused manner. "They're on acid right now."

Cathy's heart began to pound against her chest. "What?!" she cried.

Lisa nodded. "Chris told me they dropped some tabs this afternoon."

Cathy stared blankly at Lisa, hoping she was joking.

"See! I told you Jay wasn't honest with you about all the drugs he's done."

"I'm pissed," Cathy stated, realizing Lisa's intuition had—yet again—been right. She couldn't tell if she was angrier with Jason for using the drug or for hiding it from her. "Acid can make people go insane."

"It scares the crap out of me. I told Chris that he shouldn't do it anymore. He said he didn't want to, but Jay convinced him. They've done it more than once. He told me they've tripped on mescaline, too."

Cathy covered her mouth and stared at her best friend in complete awe of what she was hearing.

"Are you going to kill him?" Lisa questioned her, looking mildly entertained.

Cathy blinked before letting out a heavy breath. "It's not even worth talking to him while he's like this," she reasoned.

"Well, unfortunately, here he comes," Lisa stated and glanced warily over Cathy's shoulder.

Cathy turned around to see Jason walking toward her.

"I was wondering where you went," he said once he reached her side. He threw his arm around her shoulders without hesitation.

"Get away from me," she demanded and pushed him away from her.

Jason cocked his head to the side. "What's wrong?" he asked while stepping toward her.

"Stay away from me!" she cried and pushed him into the nearby railing. "Talk to me when you're sober."

Jason steadied himself against the railing and said, "I'm fine."

She could feel the blood boiling in her veins. She'd had enough of his half-truths. She walked toward him, stopping once her nose was only an inch away from his. She looked directly into his eyes and gave him the coldest look she could muster. "Stay away from me," she said in a firm tone before abruptly turning away from him.

"Wait!" he called out and grabbed onto her arm.

"I don't want to talk to you right now!" Cathy exclaimed angrily and wiggled free from his grip. "Not when you're like this. Enjoy the party, and I'll see you in school tomorrow."

"What's wrong with you?" he asked, eyeing her intently.

Cathy dropped her jaw. "Are you kidding? What do you think the problem is? Might it have something to do with your eyes looking black because your pupils are so dilated?"

Jason continued to hold a steady gaze on her. "I'm sorry. I thought it would wear off before you got here," he admitted. "I know you hate it when I trip."

"I hate it when you trip on 'shrooms!" Cathy yelled and stomped her foot. "*Hate* is not a strong enough word for how I feel about what you took today." She turned and walked back into the house without giving Jason a chance to respond. She could not recall ever feeling more disappointed in him.

Upon entering Chris's crowded kitchen, Cathy glanced around to see whom she could hang out with to get her mind off Jason. Bryan was talking to Jon nearby, but Cathy feared things could be awkward between her and Bryan because of Courtney. She decided to make a round through the house to see who else had shown up from her grade. As she passed by a beer pong table in the den, she heard her name. She turned around to see Luke waving her over to him. He was standing by the edge of the table with Missy and Marc.

"What's up?" Cathy asked, peering at him curiously.

"Do you want to play with us?" Luke asked. "We can do guys versus girls or you and Marc can be a team."

"I'm so bad at this game," Missy whined. "Don't make us do guys versus girls. We'll lose, no doubt."

Cathy glanced back and forth from Luke to Marc, deciding the game would be a nice distraction. "Sure. I'm up for it," she responded.

"Do you drink?" Marc asked. "We can play with water if you want."

"I drink a little," Cathy replied, "but I don't have a tolerance."

"And you're at least three shots deep," Luke reminded her. "Water might not be a bad idea."

Cathy nodded. "Water sounds good," she said and smiled at Marc. It was considerate of him to offer to play with water for her sake.

Cathy was gifted with strong hand-eye coordination, so she typically did well at games such as this. Marc was also mechanically gifted, being a star athlete and all, so she felt confident that they would win the match.

While they played, Cathy enjoyed the way Marc cheered her on every time it was her turn to shoot. At one point, he even put his hand on her back and said, "You've got this." His touch gave her butterflies. Before that moment, Jason had been the only guy ever to give her butterflies.

"You're really good at this," Marc said to Cathy after she sunk her ping pong ball into one of the remaining three cups.

"Thanks," she said and smiled brightly.

"Maybe we'd be better if we switched to water," Luke stated with a short laugh.

Missy rolled her blue eyes. "It's way less fun that way," she commented. "I'd rather lose and get drunk than win and be sober."

Luke laughed. "And that's why Marc and Cathy have this one in the bag," he remarked as he tossed Cathy and Marc back their ping pong balls. Because they had both sunk their shots, they were granted an extra turn. With only two cups remaining, they could win the game.

"Do you want to go first?" Marc asked and looked directly into Cathy's eyes.

Cathy again felt butterflies in her stomach. Marc's baby blue eyes showed her a lot about him. She saw compassion, determination, kindness, and humility. She felt blessed to have his attention because she knew many of the high school girls at the party would have loved the chance to be his teammate. She didn't have to be in high school yet to know that Marc was highly sought after by girls from all grades. "You go," she responded and smiled at him. "You'll get this," she added and squeezed his shoulder.

Marc sent her a playful smirk before tossing the ping pong ball across the table. It spun around the rim of one of the cups but then flew out of it. "I think I was a little distracted," Marc whispered to Cathy. "Your turn."

Cathy took a deep breath and switched spots with Marc. She wondered if he would touch her back again. She felt guilty about it, but she wanted him to. She assumed she was merely angry with Jason and not really interested in Marc, but at the moment, Marc had her attention.

"Get this," he said and flipped her auburn hair into her face. She pushed her hair behind her shoulder and aimed for her target. Three seconds later, her ball landed inside one of the two remaining cups.

"Nice!" Marc exclaimed and put up his hand to give her a high-five. Cathy slapped hands with him and beamed. He had significantly lifted her mood.

"Missy, we have to make our next six shots if we're going to win this," Luke said facetiously while eyeing the cups sitting in front of Marc and Cathy.

"You two don't stand a chance," Marc stated flatly.

Luke succeeded in landing his ball in a cup. Missy, however, missed her fifth shot in a row. "You really do suck at this," Luke taunted her while nudging her playfully in the side. A few seconds later, he looked up at Cathy and said, "So, where's my brother?"

Cathy flipped her hands up in the air. "No idea," she replied carelessly.

Luke looked perplexed. "Have you seen him since we got here?"

"Yup, but he decided to trip on acid tonight, so I want nothing to do with him right now," Cathy replied.

"He's tripping?" Marc asked, eyeing Cathy in disbelief.

"Him and Chris," Cathy responded.

Marc scowled, and a look of sadness filled his eyes. "Chris has been doing so well," he said with frustration. "His new girlfriend sounds like she's great for him. I've never met her, but we're all friends with her sister. I hope he doesn't mess things up with her if she comes tonight."

"Oh, she's here," Luke stated. "She came with us. Hopefully she's innocent enough not to realize he's on acid."

Marc shook his head in dismay. "Jay must have convinced him to do it," he reasoned, "because Chris told me he was all set with everything aside from weed and alcohol."

"I believe that," Cathy said. "Jason always finds a way to get exactly what he wants."

"You sound pretty pissed," Marc commented with a playful smirk.

Cathy nodded. "I told him I'd see him in school tomorrow."

Luke sighed. "He's *such* an idiot. Even I know to stick to alcohol the night before school starts."

"Enough about Jay!" Cathy cried.

"Well, are you ready to go for the win?" Marc questioned her while picking up a ping pong ball.

Cathy nodded.

"You first?" Marc asked.

Cathy shook her head.

"Okay, me first," Marc said and then centered himself with the table. The last cup was always the hardest to hit, even when playing with water. Cathy eagerly watched Marc as he threw the ball across the table. It bounced once off the rim before landing inside the cup.

"Yay!" Cathy cried. "We win!"

Marc smiled and hesitated only slightly before throwing his muscular arms around her in a celebratory embrace.

"Wait. Wait. Wait," Luke protested. "Cathy still gets a turn, and we get a rebuttal if she misses. You never know; we could go on a hot streak and sink five shots in a row."

Marc let go of Cathy and laughed loudly. "I would love to see that happen," he said in good humor. "Okay, Cathy, take your turn."

She smiled at him before stepping up to the table. Luke was doing everything he could to distract her on the other end: jumping, dancing, and waving his hands in the air. "Stop," she laughed and rolled her eyes. Luke and Missy were both laughing when Cathy finally threw her shot. Their laughter faded as it landed on top of Marc's ball inside the cup.

"Nice shot!" Marc exclaimed loudly. "Sorry, no rebuttal," he taunted

Luke and Missy.

Cathy turned toward him. "Well, that just lifted my spirits," she admitted.

"I'm sorry your boyfriend is being an idiot," Marc said.

Cathy closed her eyes and shook her head. "He's incredibly frustrating sometimes," she remarked. When she opened her eyes, Marc was gazing at her sympathetically. "But at least you guys are here," she added in a cheerful tone.

"Do you want to take some more shots of the Doctor?" Luke called to them. "They're in the freezer. There's at least four left."

Cathy eyed Luke thoughtfully, wondering if another shot would make her drunk. She felt fairly sober, perhaps just more eager to socialize. "I could probably handle one more," she reasoned, "but then I have to stop."

"They're not strong," Luke said. "I think you'll be fine."

When they entered the kitchen, Cathy noticed Lisa was engulfed in a deep conversation with Jason. They were sitting side by side on the counter near the microwave. Jason looked vested in the discussion, and Cathy wondered if they were talking about her, Chris, or the reality of time.

"Cheers to you guys kicking our butts," Luke proclaimed as he passed out nips of schnapps to Cathy, Marc, and Missy.

As Cathy opened the top of the bottle, a peppermint scent twitched her nose. "Cheers," she said and clinked her bottle with everyone else's.

"Cheers," Marc and Missy said in unison.

Cathy threw back her shot without a problem—she thought it was delicious and easy to drink. After reading the label that said it was only twenty-four percent alcohol, she reasoned she could handle another shot if Luke offered one to her. "How late are we staying?" she questioned him.

"Long enough for my brother to stop tripping, hopefully," Luke commented and glanced at Jason.

Cathy rolled her eyes.

"Are you staying here tonight, Dunkin?" Luke asked.

"No," Marc replied and shook his head. "I want to wake up in my own bed on the first day of school. I told my parents I would babysit Chris and Katie and then come home once they went to bed."

"If Chris is on acid, he won't be going to bed any time soon," Luke commented and took a deep breath. "I wonder if Courtney figured it out."

"I've barely seen Chris all night," Marc said while peering around the kitchen. "Where is he?"

"No idea," Cathy replied.

"He's probably in his bedroom," Luke gathered. "Isn't that his trademark?"

"It was with Lisa, but Courtney's different," Cathy said. "If they're in his room, then they're just talking."

"Oh, I see," Luke sang. "So, Courtney's a bit of a prude?"

Cathy laughed. "I don't know if that's the right word, but she's not Lisa."

"Are you going to talk to Jason?" Missy questioned Cathy and nodded toward him.

"I don't plan on it," Cathy replied flatly. "Talking to him is not worth my time when he's like this."

"I'm surprised he hasn't tried to steal you away from me," Marc commented and draped his arm around Cathy's shoulders. "He must see me hugging you right now."

"He's out of his mind," Cathy said matter-of-factly. "He's probably seeing yellow school buses flying around the room and purple robots talking outside the window."

Luke laughed. "Jay told me about the robots Chris 'saw.' I think they were on mescaline that time."

Cathy let out a sigh of frustration. "If you don't mind, I'd rather hang out with you guys for the rest of the night."

Marc looked at her adoringly. "Works for me," he said.

She assumed he liked the firm stance she was taking against drugs. She wondered, however, if that made her a hypocrite. After all, she had only recently stopped using Xanax, and she still ate edibles on a daily basis.

CHAPTER 10

S ITTING BESIDE JASON IN the kitchen, Lisa listened intently as he filled her in on Chris and Courtney's relationship. "It's nothing like what's between the two of you," he stressed. "They haven't done more than kiss. He isn't attracted to her the way he's attracted to you."

"Well, he seems into her," Lisa stated begrudgingly.

"You seem into Jeff," Jason responded and raised his eyebrows at her.

"I am," Lisa said flatly, "but that doesn't take away any of my feelings for Chris. It's possible to like more than one person, you know."

"Is it?"

Lisa nodded. "I like Jeff a lot, but Chris still means something to me."

"Okay, well, you still mean something to him. He's just distracting himself with Courtney right now."

Lisa loved being able to pick Jason's brain while his guard was down. "But he told me that he needed to fix himself before he could be a good boyfriend," she retorted. "Now he's *her* boyfriend. Why is he okay with dating her but not me?"

Jason sighed. "Because he loves you too much to be a burden to you. He kind of just fell into things with Courtney. If he messes up and they break up, she'll be fine. The thought of hurting you more than he already has is what drove him to break up with you. Plus, you are going through a lot with your family. The last thing you need is a screw-up for a boyfriend. Jeff is good for you because he has his act together."

"I don't want you to think I'm more interested in Chris than Jeff," Lisa said while glancing at Chris, who was standing across the kitchen with Courtney. "I just want to know if he still cares about me because I still care about him."

"He loves you as much as he always has," Jason assured her. "He likes Courtney, but he's in love with you. Like I said, he's distracting himself with her."

Lisa gazed thoughtfully in Chris's direction. Her intuition was strong, and she knew if she spent some time around him and Courtney, she would be able to tell who owned his heart. "I'm going to test the waters," she said after jumping off the counter. She took a deep breath before walking across the room. She watched Chris and Courtney's expressions as she approached them: Chris's eyes sparkled while Courtney's whole body stiffened.

"Hey!" Lisa exclaimed in a friendly manner. "Do you want to go outside and smoke?" She was not one to take school lightly, so she had planned on staying sober all night. However, if she needed to get high to shift Chris's focus back onto her, then so be it. She wanted to see if he would choose time with her over Courtney.

Chris raised his eyebrows and looked like he was at a loss for words. As Lisa peered at him, she noticed that his pupils were back to their normal size. "Um…" he stammered and locked his blue eyes on her. "I wasn't going to smoke tonight because I've been drinking, but I can pack a bowl if you want me to," he offered. "I'm sure you're probably a bit too sober for the antics going on here."

"Chris!" Courtney cried out in protest.

Lisa grinned. "That would be great!"

"It'll be fine, Court," Chris assured her. "It will just help me sleep better. Hang tight. I'll be right back," he added before turning out of the kitchen.

Courtney turned to Lisa with a sad expression on her face. "You're being a bad influence on him," she said quietly. "He's trying to stop using drugs. Why would you ask him to smoke weed?"

Lisa let out a short laugh. "Is he really *trying*, Courtney? You're extremely naïve if you think he only drank tonight."

Courtney squinted at Lisa, appearing a bit thrown off by her words.

"I know him *a lot* better than you do," Lisa said matter-of-factly. "If he didn't want to get high, he wouldn't."

"You have a new boyfriend. Why are you even here? Why can't you just leave him alone?" Courtney questioned her.

Lisa smiled slightly and shrugged. "I guess I just don't want to."

Courtney widened her blue eyes and stared at Lisa with a look of disbelief.

"Tell Chris I'll be outside," Lisa said before turning away from Courtney and walking back over to Jason.

"What was that about?" Jason asked when she reached him.

"Do you want to smoke?" she questioned him.

"Sure," Jason replied.

They were only outside for a minute before Chris and Courtney stepped onto the deck. Courtney looked less than pleased, and Lisa wondered if her sullen mood had more to do with their conversation or the marijuana in Chris's hand.

CHAPTER 11

"It's getting pretty late," Luke said to Cathy and Missy around four o'clock in the morning. "My parents will be up in an hour. We need to get out of here."

They had played multiple rounds of flip cup in the basement, and Cathy was far more buzzed than she had ever been. *Probably not the smartest thing to do before starting high school,* she thought to herself as she followed Luke and Missy out of the basement.

"Hopefully, Jay isn't passed out," Luke muttered.

Cathy rolled her eyes. After searching the first floor for Jason and Courtney, they went outside, where they saw Chris, Courtney, Lisa, and Jason. Courtney was standing beside Chris, looking rather uncomfortable. When Cathy set her eyes on Jason, she felt anger rise up inside of her. "I'll go get them," she said to Missy and Luke.

"There's my beautiful girl!" Jason cried as soon as he noticed Cathy walking toward him. Either he had forgotten they were in a fight, or he was trying to smooth things over with her.

"Courtney, we need to leave," Cathy said flatly, ignoring Jason completely.

"Don't be mad at me right before we start high school," Jason pleaded. He made his way over to her and grabbed her hand.

She immediately pulled free from his grip. "Let's go," she said assertively before abruptly turning away from him.

He grabbed onto her shoulder and pulled her back toward him.

"Stop!" she exclaimed and glared at him.

"Cathy, this is crazy. You've hidden stuff from me, and I've never gotten mad at you for it," he said defensively. "You've got to let this go."

Cathy sighed, realizing how much damage could have been done to their relationship if he had held her mistakes against her. "Let's just leave, okay?" she suggested in a calmer tone.

He immediately embraced her. "I'm sorry," he said quietly.

"I know," she muttered and begrudgingly hugged him back.

On the ride home, Missy offered Cathy shotgun—most likely to put space between her and Jason. What he had done was not just irresponsible; it was despicable.

After sneaking back inside her home, Cathy poured herself a glass of water in the kitchen and sat down at the center island. She rested her head in her hands and scolded herself for foolishly drinking twice the amount of alcohol she had ever consumed. The bus would be arriving at her house in less than three hours, and she was afraid that she would still look buzzed when her mother woke her up or—worse—that she would be sick.

After drinking two full glasses of water, Cathy climbed the two sets of stairs that led to her bedroom. Although she did not want to, she changed into her pajamas, deciding her mother would be alarmed if she found her sleeping in a sundress. She fell asleep without any problem and woke up two hours later to her mother's voice.

"Cathy! Chantal!" Mrs. Kagelli yelled from the hallway. "Time to get up!"

When Cathy opened her eyes, she felt as though she had not slept in days. She was lightheaded and woozy. As she climbed out of bed, she groaned. Functioning on autopilot, she selected the turquoise dress she had picked out the day before from her closet and threw it onto her bed. Then, hoping Chantal had not beat her to the shower, she knocked on the bathroom door. After hearing no response, she entered the bathroom while fighting to keep her eyes open. A long, hot shower would be a must, considering her pounding headache.

CHAPTER 12

An hour and a half later, Cathy was walking toward her assigned homeroom with Alyssa when Jason rushed to her side. "Can I talk to you?" he asked. His black hair was neatly spiked, and he was wearing a green-striped dress shirt with neatly ironed khakis. His blue eyes were bright and alert. He did not look like someone who had stayed up all night partying.

"Sure," Cathy replied. "Lyss, I'll catch up with you in homeroom."

"Sounds good," Alyssa said before scurrying down the hallway.

"Are we good?" Jason asked quietly, pulling her aside and peering at her in a concerned manner.

Cathy let out a heavy breath. "We'll be good if you promise never to do that again," she stated and locked her green eyes on him.

"I didn't do it to upset you."

"Promise me," she insisted.

"Fine," he acquiesced. "No more acid."

"Don't hide things from me," Cathy demanded. "Acid's dangerous! It can make people go insane!"

"Fine," he repeated, raising his voice slightly. "I'll entertain myself in ways you approve of."

Cathy sighed. "It's unfortunate that you get bored so easily."

"It is," Jason agreed.

"Just don't let me down."

"I won't," Jason promised and grabbed her hand. He squeezed it and locked his eyes on her. "Don't let me down either."

"I haven't touched Xanax since the night we… you know…"

"Good."

Cathy took a deep breath. "I didn't eat a gummy this morning because I was too afraid that I would fall asleep in school. Hopefully, I'll be too tired to get anxious about anything today."

Jason put his arm around her and led her down the hallway. "You'll be fine. We have English, bio, lunch, and computer together. Plus, you have all your other classes with Alyssa, Lisa, or Leslie. You have a good schedule."

Cathy nodded. "Thankfully."

"I have weed with me if you want to smoke later. Luke told me how to get out of here without getting caught on camera. There are some quirks in the system."

Cathy widened her eyes. The thought of smoking weed during school had never occurred to her. If they ever got caught, all the faculty members would find out about it. From the first day of school onward they would be profiled as *bad kids*. "That's way too risky," she said. "Do whatever you want but count me out."

"Will do."

"And please—whatever you do—do not tempt Chris to smoke with you," Cathy urged him. "He must be hating himself after last night."

Jason sighed. "I won't ask him to smoke. I know he needs to chill. I was pretty drunk when I talked him into tripping. I feel bad about it now."

"Well, it was his decision, so don't beat yourself up too much," Cathy stated, knowing her boyfriend tended to blame himself for other people's weaknesses.

"Thanks for not being too hard on me," Jason said quietly as they approached Cathy's homeroom. "What I did was selfish. I'm sorry."

"You were patient with me when I messed up a few weeks ago," Cathy remarked.

Jason smiled and then leaned down to kiss Cathy's forehead before dashing off toward his own homeroom. Feeling a bit envious of her boyfriend's energy, she watched him disappear into his classroom before she walked into her own.

CHAPTER 13

Later that morning as Chris entered his biology classroom beside Jason, his mind was consumed with troubling thoughts. He had woken up without any recollection of the previous night, assuming he had mixed different drugs together and finding out from Jason in homeroom that they had tripped on acid. His plan had been to only drink. Clearly, alcohol had weakened his willpower and dissolved his conviction. The worst part was, his little sister Katie had been home, and that morning, she had mentioned seeing Chris at the party. He felt incredibly ashamed. He had thought he was doing a decent job of straightening out. The previous night had been a wakeup call. He would need to make some significant changes to his lifestyle to truly clean up his act.

Chris's biology teacher allowed open seating, so he sat at a table in the back of the room with Jason, Cathy, and Leslie. He peered around the room, realizing he knew approximately half of the students in the class from sports or middle school. There was a brunette sitting toward the front of the classroom whom he noticed glance in his direction a few times. Chris could not tell if she was merely looking around to see who she knew or if she was deliberately looking at him. *She's cute,* he thought but then immediately scolded himself. *Courtney's helped me a lot. I can't let my eyes wander.* A flirt by nature, Chris could not help but smile at the girl the next time he noticed her looking his way. She immediately dropped her eyes to the floor, and he hoped he hadn't embarrassed her.

***

Later that morning, Cathy and Lisa were sitting in their Algebra II class, trying their hardest not to fall asleep. "I deliberately came between Chris and Courtney last night," Lisa admitted quietly to Cathy while their teacher, Mr. Jackson, took attendance. "I'm a horrible person sometimes."

"What did you do?" Cathy asked curiously.

"I asked him to smoke weed, even though I didn't want to get high," Lisa replied. "Courtney called me a bad influence. She had no idea he was tripping."

"You talked to Courtney?"

"Briefly. I told her she was naïve to believe he was only drinking."

"You're bad."

"I know. I feel kind of bad."

"I can't believe you feel bad!"

"Well, what if Chris regrets getting high and resents me for it?" Lisa asked.

"I doubt he remembers much," Cathy gathered. "He was on a lot of different things."

"I need to keep my distance from him," Lisa concluded. "I don't want Courtney to become his inspiration and me to be his demise."

"You're not going to be his *demise*," Cathy stated and rolled her eyes. "Why are you being so dramatic?"

"I need to leave the past in the past and focus on Jeff," Lisa resounded. "He's good to me, and he's got everything going for him. If I stop thinking about Chris, I'm sure I'll fall in love with Jeff. He's gorgeous and smart. There's nothing not to love about him."

"So, do that," Cathy said. "Jason and I think Jeff's better for you, anyway."

"Do you know his parents put him in modeling when he was a child? He was actually in some clothing ads."

"I'm not surprised," Cathy admitted. Jeff was one of the best-looking guys in their grade. He had bright blue eyes, warm-blonde hair, and an all-American-boy air about him.

"He's everything I told you I wanted last year," Lisa said.

"I know, and you didn't want to enter high school as Chris's girlfriend," Cathy recounted. "You're lucky he broke up with you. You and Jeff will be a power couple in no time."

"Just like you and Jay," Lisa agreed.

Cathy rolled her eyes and shook her head. "Honestly, we're less than stable," she confessed. "Last night, Marc Dunkin gave me butterflies."

Lisa widened her olive-green eyes and raised her eyebrows.

"I'm sure I was just mad at Jay," Cathy added.

"Marc's hot, but he's not worth messing things up with Jay over," Lisa asserted. "I doubt he'd ever consider dating a freshman—even one as pretty as you."

Cathy blushed. "All I'm saying is that Jay really upset me last night. What kind of moron takes acid on a school night?"

Lisa let out a short laugh. "One who can depend on Adderall for energy the next day."

Cathy sighed. Jason was beginning to concern her. When she had fallen in love with him, he had been sober and responsible. Something had driven him to begin experimenting with drugs, to resume taking Adderall, and to start drinking. She feared she might have been the catalyst—considering her anxiety, depression, and dysfunctional relationship with Chantal. She had leaned on Jason for support, and since seventh grade, he had been taking all of her problems onto his shoulders. Moreover, he had spent all of his free time with her, likely losing a part of himself in the process. *Could I be ruining him?*

Mr. Jackson began passing out copies of the syllabus, thankfully diverting Cathy's attention away from her depressing analysis. "This is an honors course," he said to the class. "You will have a project every term and homework every night. An A in this course will not give you a 4.0; it will give you a 4.5. You're going to end up working really hard for those extra points, but that's how you'll get into college. You are only here because your previous math teacher thought you were one of his or her top students. Congratulations, someone thinks you're smart. Now, prove it to me."

CHAPTER 14

Before lunch, Jason met Cathy at her locker so they could attempt to find the cafeteria together. Although Montgomery Lake High was only the home of six-hundred students, it was quite large and spread out in design. The school was split up into two "houses"—red for the underclassmen and blue for the upperclassmen. Each house resided in its own wing of the building, and the shared facilities were centralized. A large gymnasium with an indoor track, a cafeteria with a courtyard, and a state-of-the-art auditorium were some of the school's best features. Montgomery was an affluent town, and its taxpayers poured money into the school system. For that reason, MLH was typically ranked within the top ten public high schools in Massachusetts year after year.

"Let's just head towards the front entrance," Jason suggested. "Everyone's walking that way, so the cafeteria must be near there."

Cathy nodded and closed her locker. "How do you like your classes so far?" she asked as she began walking with him through the crowded hall.

"Well, you were in half of them, but the other two were kind of strange," he replied. "It's weird having geometry with sophomores and Latin with upperclassmen. My math teacher probably thinks I'm a sophomore, but I look really out of place in Latin. Some of my brothers' friends are in my class."

"Well, that's what a St. Timothy's education does for people—puts them way ahead of the standard curriculum. How many years have you taken

Latin?"

"Five."

"Are there any other freshmen in those classes?"

"Katherine Rossi."

"I'm not surprised. She's wicked smart."

Jason nodded. "She is. Unfortunately, she seems to hate me."

"We've been over this. She's stuck up," Cathy remarked, hoping Katherine's attitude would not faze him.

"Right… well… on another note, I had an interesting conversation with Chris earlier. Lunch might be a little awkward. You know how he invited everyone back over his house for tomorrow night?"

"Yeah."

"Well, he's going to call off the party."

"Why?"

"Exactly what you said this morning," Jason replied. "He's beating himself up over what happened last night."

"Is he beating himself up or is Courtney beating him up?" Cathy wondered aloud.

"I don't know, but he's acting strange. I told him I'd cover for him and invite everyone to my house. Luke's having a party. It will be fun."

"Hmmm… I wonder if it's him or Courtney who doesn't want the party."

"Chris said she really wants to become friends with you."

Cathy sighed. "It's just awkward because of Bryan and Lisa. I don't want to be mean to Courtney, but by being nice to her, I'm being mean to them."

"Bryan won't hold it against you. Lisa's another story."

"I want to figure out who's behind the party being cancelled," Cathy said as they approached the cafeteria. "Chris has never done that before, so either he's extra serious about straightening out or Courtney's putting pressure on him."

"I think Courtney wants to party with us," Jason stated. "I've seen a mischievous sparkle in her eyes on a few occasions, and I think she had Chris in mind when she ended things with Bryan."

"Really?"

Jason nodded. "You know I enjoy reading people."

"What do you think she likes better about Chris than Bryan?"

"Chris is the life of the party. I'm not calling Court shallow, but I think she wanted to start off high school 'popular.'"

"Bryan's popular!" Cathy cried defensively.

"Yeah, but he kept her away from our friends," Jason said.

Cathy cocked her head to the side in thought. "Hmmm… you could be onto something. I'll do some digging at lunch. Jon, Lyss, and Chris are over there," she said and pointed across the cafeteria towards her friends, who were about to sit down at a rectangular table.

"You don't want to sit with Lisa?"

"I told her I didn't want to sit with Andy and Chantal," Cathy replied. "She understood. They don't accept us."

CHAPTER 15

CATHY LOCKED HER GREEN eyes on Courtney as she approached Cathy's lunch table. Just like the previous night, Courtney was dressed nicely and wearing a lot of makeup. Cathy could not judge Courtney for changing her style to fit in because she had done the exact same thing in seventh grade when she allowed Lisa to give her a makeover.

A few seconds later, Courtney sat down beside Chris. "Hi, guys," she greeted everyone. "What's up?"

"Hi, Court," Chris replied with a wide grin.

"Hey, Court! This is Alyssa!" Jon exclaimed. He sounded excited to introduce them, which led Cathy to believe Jon liked Courtney a lot. Alyssa was sitting diagonally across from Courtney, sandwiched between Cathy and Jon.

"Hi!" Courtney cried in a warm tone. "I'm Courtney, Chris's girlfriend."

"Right," Alyssa said and then turned to Cathy. "Did the guys not tell her that we're practically related?" she whispered.

Cathy let out a short laugh, wondering if Jon or Chris had even thought to tell Courtney that Alyssa's brother was dating her own sister.

Alyssa turned back to Courtney and stated, "Your sister dates my brother."

"John Kelly is your brother?" Courtney asked.

Alyssa nodded.

"My sister told me he had a sister, but she never said more than that,"

Courtney remarked. "Small world!"

Cathy's eyes widened as she watched Bryan sit down on the other side of Courtney.

"Hi, Courtney," he greeted her.

"Hi," she replied, turning towards him. "How's it going, Bryan?"

"Not too bad," he said and smiled awkwardly. "Hi, Chris."

"Hey," Chris answered rather lifelessly from the other side of Courtney. "Have fun last night?"

Bryan glared at Chris. "Did you?" he retorted.

Chris shrugged. "I don't know. Did I?" he asked, turning toward Courtney.

Courtney nodded and smiled. "Of course you did! Why else would you have invited everyone back for tomorrow night?"

"Is that what you want?" Chris asked with a hesitant smile.

Courtney looked confused. "Why does it matter what I want?" she questioned him. "It's your house."

"I thought you said the party was off?" Jason called out loudly from beside Cathy.

"Off?" their friends questioned Chris in unison.

Chris widened his eyes, seeming startled by Jason's statement. "Well, I don't know," he responded uneasily and then looked down at the table. "Maybe it's... it's just better if... I don't want... I just have to call it off."

Cathy eyed him precariously. The boy sitting diagonally across from her was not the Chris she knew. He sounded conflicted, whereas Chris always seemed so confident. "What's with you lately?" Cathy questioned him and raised her eyebrows in a confused manner. "You've been acting weird ever since you hooked up with Courtney. Did your girlfriend brainwash you or something?"

Jason immediately nudged Cathy in the side, letting her know she had gone a bit too far. She hadn't meant to sound accusatory; she was just sleep-deprived and curious. Courtney turned bright red, and Cathy immediately regretted speaking so frankly.

"Don't bring her into this," Chris demanded and stood up from his seat. "I don't want to have the party. Maybe I'm sick of having my house trashed and my family mad at me. Can you comprehend that possibility?"

"Whatever," Cathy said, trying her best to appear unmoved as she darted her eyes from Chris to Courtney. "Maybe you don't want a party, but Courtney might," she added in a friendly tone, hoping she had not offended Courtney with her unintentionally brash statement.

"Of course she does," Alyssa concluded. "I can tell just by looking at her that she's no low life. Right, Court?" Alyssa, who was all about bringing people together, most likely felt bad that Courtney had been put on the spot.

"Right," Courtney agreed and smiled.

Courtney's smile brought Cathy an immense amount of relief. "I told you she was just like us," she said to Alyssa, hoping to put Courtney further to ease. She could not help but notice that Chris looked extremely perturbed by her and Alyssa's comments.

"Listen up, guys. If Chris doesn't have a party tomorrow night, you can count on one at my place," Jason said. "My parents are going out of town, and they're leaving Matt in charge. Luke has already started throwing out invites. It should be a good time."

"You realize your brother is out of control, don't you?" Alyssa remarked, *clearly* referring to Luke. "He's going to invite everyone he sees. The entire school is going to show up at your house."

"My night won't be ruined if you stay home," Jason teased her. He coughed twice and laughed before playfully winking at her.

Alyssa glared at him, appearing offended. She took more crap from Jason, Bryan, and Chris than anyone did because they all treated her like a sister. "Come on, Courtney," she said, "let's go dump our trays."

After Courtney followed Alyssa across the cafeteria, Jason turned to Cathy and asked, "Why the *hell* did you say that about Courtney?!"

Cathy let out a heavy breath. "I'm sorry," she said to her boyfriend before tapping Chris on the arm. "Hey, Chris, I'm sorry. I wasn't trying to make her feel uncomfortable. It came out of my mouth before I even knew I was speaking."

"It's fine," Chris said flatly without looking her in the eye. "We're all a bit sleep deprived and on edge."

Cathy thought Chris looked more exhausted than Bryan, Jon, or anyone else who had attended the party. She assumed that meant he had not taken any drugs before school; otherwise, he would have appeared wide awake like Jason. Locking her eyes on Chris, she could not shake the feeling that he had finally hit rock-bottom.

CHAPTER 16

When the last bell of the day rang, the relief Jason felt was immense. As excited as he had been to finally attend high school with his friends, the day had dragged on way too long. Staying up until five o'clock in the morning had been a terrible idea. He assumed his friends were feeling even more drained than him because they had not taken Adderall. Jason could not wait to find Matt, get a ride home, and pass out for hours—if he could actually fall asleep. Somehow, he found his way to the senior parking lot, where his brother had parked that morning.

"You're such an idiot," Matt called out to him as soon as their blue eyes met.

"What?" Jason questioned him, escaping from a daze.

"Did you think I wouldn't hear about last night?" Matt asked. He was leaning against his Lexus SUV beside his girlfriend Ally.

Jason widened his eyes, wondering what Matt had heard.

"How are you even functioning right now?" Matt questioned him while raising his eyebrows.

Jason dropped his backpack to the ground as he reached the car. "What did you hear?"

"Everything," Matt replied.

"So, you know Luke and I stayed out late?"

Matt widened his eyes, and Jason assumed his brother knew a lot more than that. "Just get in the car before I kill you," Matt stated angrily.

Jason sighed and climbed into the backseat.

"If you took a drug-test right now, what would show up in your system, Jay?" Matt questioned him after backing out of his parking spot.

Jason scowled. "What did you hear?" he asked impatiently.

Matt let out a short laugh. "You were at a party with my best friend, who had to entertain your girlfriend—all night—because you decided to trip on acid. Acid?! What the hell is wrong with you?!"

"I don't know," Jason replied carelessly and rested his head against the window. He closed his eyes and wished Matt would stop talking.

"What am I supposed to do with this information?" Matt questioned him crossly. "Tell Mom and Dad to get you drug-tested? Beat the crap out of you? Kill Luke for being a bad influence?"

"Ugh, God. Do whatever you want. I don't care," Jason whined. "I feel like absolute ass."

"The problem is you should have felt like this all day long, but you didn't," Matt said suspiciously. "I saw you this morning, and I saw you during lunch—you were fine. Your friends? Not so fine. What did you take to get yourself through the day?"

"Just Adderall," Jason replied immediately without opening his eyes.

"How much?" Matt pressed.

"Obviously not enough," Jason retorted.

"Why are you doing this? Why are you following Luke's footsteps instead of mine?"

Jason shot his blue eyes wide open; he had never thought of it like that. He had always admired Matt—not Luke. "I'm not following Luke anywhere," he stated defensively. "Luke's going to hell in a handbasket."

Matt let out a frustrated groan and slammed his hands against the steering wheel. Jason had never seen him look so angry.

"I look up to *you*, not Luke," Jason stated emphatically.

"Your actions suggest otherwise," Ally, who was sitting shotgun, said quietly.

"You're right," Jason admitted, hoping they would both leave him alone.

"Do you think I don't know what Luke does?" Matt asked.

"I have no idea what you know," Jason replied.

"He drinks and drives; he vapes; he rolls on ecstasy and molly; he does coke!" Matt exclaimed. "Luke is a disaster, but I'm more worried about *you*. I've been more worried about you than him all year because you are—usually—smart enough to not get caught doing anything wrong. So, why did you let me catch you smoking weed?"

Jason was thrown off by his brother's question. "What?"

"Why did you take acid, knowing I would find out?" Matt pressed.

Jason sat in silence, unsure of how to answer his brother's questions.

"You're too smart to get caught, JD. It's as simple as that—but you're getting yourself caught," Matt continued.

"Well, then, maybe I'm not as smart as you think I am," Jason responded.

"Bullshit. We both know that's not true," Matt said. "So, what you need to do is figure out the answer to my question. *Why* do you want to get caught?"

"I don't want to get caught."

"There is something wrong with you," Matt stated in a somber tone. "I don't know if it's the Adderall Mom and Dad force you to take, which you don't need. I don't know if it's your friends or your pretty little girlfriend. I don't know what is influencing you, but the person you are today is not the kid I've known or the brother I've loved for the last fourteen years."

Jason rested his head in his hands and sighed, realizing Matt was doing to him what he had once done to Cathy. He was trying to get Jason to see that drugs were changing his character.

"You are Mom and Dad's pride and joy," Matt stated without any resentment. "You've always loved being the 'favorite child'—the one who got to go to the expensive middle school, the one they brag about all the time. But right now, you would risk breaking their hearts by letting them find out about what you did last night. Wow. That is *insane* to me. That is not you. You, Jason? You care about things. You care about *everything*. You care about *everyone*, so the apathetic person sitting in my backseat right now is not *you*."

Jason sat in silence, stunned by Matt's outburst. He assumed it would have deeply bothered him to see his brother so upset if he weren't completely exhausted.

"What can you tell me?" Matt questioned him.

"About what?" Jason asked.

"Anything I've mentioned!" Matt yelled.

"My brain is mush right now," Jason replied matter-of-factly. "I can't process everything you just said. I'm sure it will register by tomorrow. I'm just beat from staying up all night."

"Mom and Dad are going to a wedding in Nantucket tomorrow and leaving me in charge," Matt said. "I will not let you out of the house or one friend of yours into our house until you come up with some answers."

"Okay," Jason agreed and rubbed his aching head. "I'm sure I'll have all the answers tomorrow."

When Jason got home, he crawled upstairs to his bedroom. After changing into a t-shirt and gym shorts, he climbed into his bed and threw his baby-blue down comforter over his head, hoping he would be able to sleep. An hour later, he was still restlessly tossing and turning. He heard his cell phone begin to vibrate on his nightstand, so he looked to see who was calling: Chris. Jason let out a heavy breath, realizing he was far too brain-fried to answer the phone. He climbed out of bed, deciding that trying to fall asleep naturally was a lost cause. He was too exhausted to venture outside to smoke weed, so he hoped Luke had some edibles.

Luke was not home, but he had shown Jason where he kept his stash—inside a safe in his closet. After entering a four-digit code, Jason opened the safe, reaching past documents and money, to sift through various bags of weed and bottles of pills. Unfortunately, he found no edibles. He wondered if Luke kept them in a cooler somewhere. Then he remembered Luke had a fridge in his room. Unfortunately, the fridge was filled only with water bottles, cheese, and Red Bull. Desperately, Jason went back over to the safe and began reading the bottles, checking to see if Luke had any sedatives. Each bottle was labeled in black marker, but Jason knew he could not trust the labels to be accurate. He found a bottle marked "ZX" and opened it up. He poured a few blue, oval pills into his hand. The Xanax Luke had given Cathy was white, so either these were not Xanax or they were a different dosage.

Jason walked across the room to sit down at Luke's computer. He quickly googled the number on the pills to find out what he was holding in his hand. They were, in fact, Xanax—one milligram each. As much as he hated the idea of taking a benzo, he was desperate for sleep. He walked back over to Luke's closet, closed the safe, and left the room with three milligrams.

When he reached his bedroom, he felt a pang of guilt. He was about to do exactly what he had made Cathy promise not to do. "#$%&," he said out loud. "I'm pathetic." He fell back onto his bed and considered his options. He reasoned that taking one dose of Xanax would not get him addicted; however, he would feel terrible hiding it from Cathy. If she ever found out, she could start using it again. Jason let out a heavy breath. He couldn't do it. Although Xanax would surely put him to sleep, he had to find another way.

He opened a bottle of Tylenol that was on his desk and dropped the three blue pills into it. Then he reached into his desk drawer and pulled out a bag of weed and his bowl. He knew it was risky to open his window and smoke in his bedroom since Matt was home, but he was desperate. After taking five or six large hits, Jason felt his mind and body begin to relax. He let out a sigh of relief, knowing he would quickly fall asleep.

CHAPTER 17

Jason woke up the following morning around six o'clock, after sleeping for over twelve hours. As he sat up, his mind began flooding with Matt's questions from the previous day. Sadly, it had never even occurred to him that Marc would tell Matt that he had tripped on acid. Furthermore, he had never considered the possibility of Matt telling their parents. Such news would surely devastate them, considering they had given Jason every possible blessing a parent could provide. Although he did not have to get up for twenty minutes, he climbed out of bed and went downstairs. He could not believe how much better he felt after a solid night's rest.

"Good morning, Jay. Are you feeling better?" his mother asked the second she spotted him enter the kitchen.

"Much better," Jason replied and walked over to their industrial-sized, stainless-steel refrigerator. After pouring himself a glass of orange juice, he made his way over to the granite island in the middle of the room.

"Matt said you looked sick when you guys left school yesterday," his mother commented and raised her eyebrows at him in a concerned manner.

Jason nodded, finding it difficult to look her in the eye. "I didn't get much sleep the night before school started. I've been having trouble sleeping lately. I think my dose of Adderall is too high."

His mother cocked her head to the side. "You just slept for half a day," she said matter-of-factly.

"Right. Because I only slept for two hours the night before."

"How often has that been happening to you?"

"Honestly? It's been happening a lot. Can you ask my doctor if I can take a smaller dose? I think I might have to be weaned down or switched to a different medication."

Mrs. Davids nodded. "I'll call his office on my way into work. It's just strange that this never happened to you before. You've been on it for years."

Jason shrugged. "Maybe I just don't need as much of it anymore?"

"Yeah, maybe. I would hate for your grades to slip, though. It really counts now, but obviously you need to sleep."

"My grades won't slip, Mom," Jason assured her.

"You feel better now?" she asked.

Jason nodded.

"Well, I have a quiche in the oven that will be ready in ten minutes. Why don't you hop in the shower and then come back down for breakfast?"

"Sure thing," Jason replied, happy that his mother was willing to talk to his doctor. He was only prescribed fifteen milligrams of Adderall per day, but he had been taking double that—or more—for the last few months. Now, however, he wanted to wean himself off of it completely. He assumed his mother would not be on board with that, but regardless of what his doctor recommended, Jason planned to take less and less of it until he no longer needed it at all.

An hour later, Jason met Matt in the foyer and silently followed him outside to his car, dreading their impending conversation. "I hope you have answers for me," Matt said as soon as he shut the driver's side door.

"I do," Jason replied as Matt began backing out of the driveway. "I don't think I need to be on Adderall. It's messing up my sleep schedule, and I can't think straight. I talked to Mom before breakfast, and she said she'll ask my doctor to lower my dose. I've hardly slept more than three hours a night in the last month. I honestly didn't even consider the consequences of you finding out that I had tripped. I can't think straight when I'm sleep deprived."

"Okay, decent answer to *one* of my questions," Matt remarked, "but that doesn't explain why you let me catch you smoking weed a few months ago."

Jason sighed. "Yeah, it does. Adderall makes me too jittery, so I smoke weed to calm myself down. Maybe I subconsciously thought if I got caught then Mom and Dad would take me off Adderall? I don't like smoking weed. I would rather eat it, honestly, but it's the only way I can regulate my body. I'm going to ask around to see if anyone can get me edibles until I'm off Adderall. I can keep them in a cooler in my room."

"Ask Luke," Matt muttered. "He seems to have the hookup on everything these days."

"Do you know who he gets stuff from?" Jason asked, wondering if Matt knew Luke was dealing drugs or if he just thought Luke had a friend who did.

"Nope," Matt replied. "I want nothing to do with that situation. Luke needs to learn how to be responsible for his own actions. If he gets in trouble, he deserves it."

"Do you think Luke is dealing or just buying stuff from a friend?" Jason asked curiously.

"Does it make a difference? Whether he makes money or not he's still providing kids we know with drugs. Half of my friends party pretty hard. They've all told me Luke's the one with the hookup. None of them have asked him where the stuff comes from, but he's gotten them plenty of MDMA and coke."

"I didn't realize your friends partied *that* hard," Jason admitted, wondering who Matt was referring to.

"That's because my closest friends don't touch drugs," Matt stated matter-of-factly as they pulled up to Ally's house. He put the SUV in park and turned towards Jason. "So, you're telling me that you need weed to counteract Adderall?"

"Yeah."

"And where does acid come into play?"

Jason let out a heavy breath. "That was a result of me being bored and not thinking straight because I was sleep deprived. It was a very bad decision."

"Marc said Cathy was pretty pissed at you."

"Yeah. She made me promise never to do it again."

"I think he liked hanging out with her," Matt said while waiting for Ally to climb into the car.

Jason rolled his eyes. "Marc's a flirt. Cathy isn't."

"Keep your $%#& together or you're going to lose that girl," Matt warned him.

"She's not as innocent as she seems," Jason remarked.

"Well, who's to blame for that?" Matt asked rhetorically.

CHAPTER 18

CHRIS ARRIVED AT SCHOOL that morning with a lot on his mind. He made his way to his own locker before anxiously waiting at Jason's. He had tried to get ahold of Jason three or four times the previous night but had been unsuccessful. When he saw Jason heading toward him, he took a deep breath. He had no idea how their conversation was going to go. Jason was typically rational and understanding, but he had been acting a bit out of character lately.

"Hey. What's up, man?" Jason greeted him casually when he reached his locker.

"Hey, did you get my messages last night?" Chris asked.

Jason widened his eyes. "I did this morning. Sorry, dude. I passed out right after school."

"Yeah, I figured," Chris said downheartedly.

"What's up?" Jason asked, looking Chris up and down.

Chris took a deep breath. "I'm not coming to your party tonight," he blurted out.

Jason cocked his head to the side and squinted. "Is Courtney being hard on you because of the other night?"

"No," Chris replied and shook his head. "She's planning to go to your house with Alyssa."

"Really?"

"I have to take a break," Chris admitted. "I can't hang out with people who party hard if I want to sober up. I'm too weak. I can't handle it."

"What? You've been doing great."

Chris widened his eyes. "Yeah, maybe until the other night."

Jason sighed. "I'm sorry about that. I wasn't thinking straight. Matt laid into me hard about it, and he made a lot of sense."

"Marc laid into me, but even if he hadn't, I would have come to the same conclusion," Chris said. "I need to stay away from certain people right now, including you."

Jason looked taken aback. "What, dude?"

"I'm too easily tempted to get high or drunk. I can't be around it, or I'll never get my act together."

"Well, you don't have to stop hanging out with *me*. I just won't drink or get high around you."

"You don't get it. We've been partying together for a while. I associate you with a lot of things I am trying to put in the past. I need a break, Jay. Not forever. Hopefully not even for long—just long enough to find some strength."

Jason looked as though the wind had been knocked out of him, and Chris felt terrible. Realizing that Jason was a bad influence on him had been rather painful. Jason was the closest thing Chris had to a brother. Putting space between them was going to be one of the hardest things Chris had ever done, but he knew he needed to do it—not just for himself but for Jason as well. They brought out the worst in each other.

"I wouldn't even smoke weed if it wasn't for you," Jason retorted. "You're the one who begged me to try things. You told me to snort Adderall to get high. You said it was a lot of fun. Well, you know what? It's not fun anymore. I haven't snorted it in a while, but I'm still one hundred percent addicted to it. I can't even sleep at night."

"And that is exactly why we need to stay away from each other," Chris said in a serious tone. "I bring out the worst in you. I got you into drugs. I'm a bad friend, but I realize it now. I couldn't see it before. I thought we were just having fun. I'm sorry."

"You don't have to be sorry; just don't blame me for your problems," Jason remarked.

Chris let out a heavy breath. "I'm not blaming you. I'm blaming myself. I'm trying to help both of us." He did not mean to sound frustrated, but he could not understand why Jason was not hearing him.

"Fine, Chris," Jason said and threw his hands up in the air. "Go hibernate with Courtney, Jon, and whoever else you haven't corrupted yet."

Chris dropped his jaw. "See? You blame me."

"That's not what I meant," Jason retracted.

"But you said it," Chris stated matter-of-factly.

Jason sighed.

"You can't blame me without thinking I'm right," Chris retorted. "I corrupted you, Bryan, and Jon; I ruined Chantal and Jon's relationship; I came between Courtney and Bryan; I hurt Lisa; I'm sure I've caused fights between you and Cathy. In the name of fun, I got you all to do things you would never have done without me in your lives."

Jason rolled his eyes. "Dude, you are being *way* too dramatic. The other night was a dumb move. I agree. It was a horrible decision on my part. I knew you were trying to stay away from drugs, but I got drunk and made a bad choice. You did, too. Lesson learned. I'm not going to turn my back on my best friend because we tripped on acid together. I'm not going to blame you for my bad choices. We're in this together."

"I'm asking you to give me some time; that's all," Chris said. "Can you do that?"

"Who are you trying to help? Me or you?" Jason questioned him.

"Both of us," Chris replied matter-of-factly.

"Best friends are supposed to stick together—not turn away from each other when things get hard," Jason stated.

"I just need some time to get my head on straight," Chris said. "I hope someday you'll understand and forgive me."

Jason lowered his eyebrows and squinted at him in a perplexed manner.

"I'm sorry, guy," Chris added and patted Jason on the shoulder before walking away from him. More than anything, he wished Jason could see where he was coming from. The pain in his best friend's eyes brought tears to his own. As Chris moved through the corridor towards his homeroom, he did everything he could to stop himself from crying.

He had not spoken to Courtney since the previous day, and he was less than excited to see her. Although she had served as a catalyst of positive change in his life, her priorities had become askew. It seemed to Chris as though she had used him to get to know his friends—everyone whom Bryan had kept from her. When Chris saw how excited Courtney was to get ready with Alyssa for Jason's party, he realized she was on a quest for popularity.

The only reason Chris knew he was considered "popular" was because no one else seemed to be. There was no other group he wished he were a part of and no "hotter" spot to hang out at in Montgomery than his house. It had been that way since Taylor was in high school. Chris was smart enough to realize his own popularity had nothing to do with his character but everything to do with his connection to the older kids. Without Jordan, Taylor, Marc, or Jason's brothers, Chris would never have been able to host the gatherings that gave him his "life of the party" reputation. Popularity had been handed to him on a silver platter. It was something Taylor and Jordan had earned by being powerhouses on the football field. It had been passed onto Marc and his friends by default and later onto Chris. After much reflection, Chris realized that the world had told him who he was before he could even ask himself the question.

CHAPTER 19

JASON STRUGGLED TO CALM his heart rate as he walked through the freshmen locker hall. He was in awe of what had just happened between him and Chris, and he needed to talk to Cathy as soon as possible. He had planned to tell her about his conversation with Matt as soon as he saw her, but now the situation with Chris was at the forefront of his mind. His stomach was in knots; his heart was pounding against his chest; and he thought he might be having his first anxiety attack.

Thankfully, Jason and Chris were not assigned seats beside each other in homeroom. Although their last names were alphabetically close, four students sat between them. When Jason entered the room, Chris did not look in his direction. As Jason planted his eyes on him, he thought of how awkward third-period biology would be. Thankfully, he had first period English with Cathy, so he could fill her in on what had transpired. Jason's whole body felt shaky—not in a jittery sense but in a weak one. He honestly had never before felt the emotions he was feeling. He wondered if it was how Cathy had felt when Chantal cut her out of her life. He did not know if he was sad or angry, but he knew he was confused.

Twenty minutes later, he sat beside Cathy in their English classroom, explaining everything to her.

"I could tell yesterday that Chris was hitting rock-bottom," she whispered once Jason finished speaking. "He was doing well, but then he fell back into his old ways with minimal pressure from you. I think it showed him how weak he truly is. Based on what he said to you, I don't think he's blaming you or that he's mad at you; I think he just really wants to get sober. Plenty of people can stay sober around others who aren't, but Chris can't."

Jason hung his head. "I want him to figure out his $%&#. I do. I want what's best for him, but I can't help feeling like he's ditching me."

"Mr. Davids and Miss Kagelli, please stop talking," their English teacher, Mr. Blackwell, said with slight frustration. "You are supposed to be reading on your iPads."

Jason cleared his throat. "I'm sorry, Mr. B. I already read it, but I didn't mean to be disruptive," he said. The last thing he wanted to do was get on any of his teachers' bad sides. Regardless of how much Matt thought his personality had changed, Jason still cared as much about getting straight A's as always.

"It's okay, Jason," Mr. Blackwell responded. "Just let everyone else finish reading in silence."

Jason nodded and smiled sheepishly at his teacher before opening up the Messenger app on his iPad. The high school had provided each student with an iPad to use for the year, so Jason and Cathy finally had a way to text each other.

Jason: Sorry I got you in trouble

Cathy: You saved face per usual. I have to finish reading that passage. I'll message you when I'm done.

Jason: Sounds good

While Cathy read a scene from *Romeo and Juliet* that Jason had read in middle school, he fretted about seeing Chris during biology and lunch. He wondered who else Chris was going to cut out of his life. Was Bryan straightedge enough to remain his friend? Were Chris and Bryan even on speaking terms? Who was Chris going to hang out with? Jon and Courtney were the only straightedge kids in their group. Jason doubted Chantal and Andy's friends would welcome Chris into their clique, considering Chris's complicated relationship with Lisa. Was he planning to completely isolate himself? Chris was the most social person Jason knew. What was he thinking?

In biology, Chris acted as though nothing were wrong. He sat at the same table as Jason and conducted the lab without displaying any unusual emotions. When Leslie brought up the party, Chris did not say anything about not going.

During lunch, however, a small incident occurred: Courtney and Chris got into an argument in the middle of the cafeteria's courtyard. None of their friends seemed fazed by the tension between them. Bryan actually seemed pleased, and Jason couldn't blame him.

Shortly after the conflict, Alyssa informed everyone that Chris and Courtney had argued over the party. "He isn't going, and he doesn't want her to go either," she reported with a genuinely perplexed expression on her face. This, of course, confused everyone. A few moments later, Chris returned to the table to retrieve his belongings. He offered no explanation before leaving the area.

"Sartelli and Anderson!" Jason called out after Chris had walked away.

Bryan and Jon turned toward him, both looking dumbfounded by Chris's behavior.

"Do you want to come to my house to pregame after school?" Jason asked.

"Sure," Bryan replied.

"All right," Jon agreed, sounding a bit surprised that Jason had invited him. Although Jon, Jason, Chris, and Bryan were "best friends," Jason and Jon had not been close since Jon's breakup with Chantal. Nevertheless, Jason realized he needed to hang onto his friends while he still could. Clearly, Chris had not cut the cord from anyone else, for if he had, people would not be so surprised by what had just happened.

After school, Matt had football practice, so Luke offered to drive Jason and Cathy home. With football season beginning, Matt would be tied up after school for the foreseeable future, meaning Jason would have to depend on either Luke or the bus for a ride home every day.

"How many people did you invite tonight?" Jason questioned Luke as they drove across Montgomery. Cathy was in the backseat beside Jason, and Missy was sitting shotgun.

"Mainly just seniors," Luke replied. "I mentioned it to a couple of kids in my grade who are on the football team with Matt. I'm sure he invited some people, just like you did."

"I didn't invite anyone besides my close friends," Jason said. "Chris isn't even coming."

"Why not?" Luke asked.

Jason sighed. "He just needs to chill for a bit."

Luke laughed. "I can see that."

"What are you planning to do at the party?" Jason asked curiously.

"What do you mean?" Luke questioned him.

"Like, are you getting drugs, or are you just going to drink?" Jason clarified.

"Why? Are you looking for drugs?" Luke responded.

"I don't know," Jason replied. "I was just wondering what your plan is." Although he wanted to wean himself off Adderall and eventually stop smoking weed, Jason decided tonight was not the best night to begin that journey. He was feeling a bit heartbroken and in no mood to party. If he was going to host his friends, then he would need something to take off the edge.

"Well, I have some hard liquor and a few beer balls in my trunk," Luke said. "I know you have weed, so what else would you be looking for?"

"Nothing," Jason replied immediately. "I was just curious." When he had searched Luke's safe, he saw Luke's collection of drugs: molly, weed, Adderall, Xanax, Klonopin, and Vicodin. Despite what Matt mentioned about coke, Luke did not appear to have any. Jason wondered if Matt had exaggerated or if Luke had really gone that far. "Have you tried coke?" he asked a few seconds later, unable to contain his curiosity.

Cathy shot Jason a strange look, and he assumed she was wondering why he would ever think that.

"You're not doing coke, Jay-dawg," Luke replied with a short laugh.

"That's not what I asked," Jason responded matter-of-factly. "I don't want to do coke. Adderall is basically cheap coke, and I wish I was never prescribed it."

Cathy, again, shot Jason a look of surprise. He had not yet told her about his conversation with Matt.

"Matt told me you did coke. I'm asking if it's true," Jason clarified.

Luke scowled. "Why the hell would he say that?"

"We had an honest talk yesterday. He was upset that I tripped at Chris's party," Jason replied.

Cathy, for the third time, shot Jason a surprised look.

"I've tried coke, but I don't 'do' it," Luke said. "The only thing I like to do besides drink is roll. I have plenty of benzos, weed, and painkillers, but I don't 'do' them."

"So, are you rolling tonight?" Jason asked.

"I don't know," Luke replied, "but you're definitely not."

Jason let out a heavy breath. "I'm not asking for ecstasy."

"Well, you said you don't know if you want drugs, so what am I supposed to think? What might you want, Jay?"

"Nothing. Forget it," Jason replied immediately. "I was just curious because of what Matt said yesterday." He glanced over at Cathy, who looked dumbfounded by the entire conversation.

When they arrived at his house, she asked him about his talk with Matt. "Matt's a good brother," she said after Jason explained everything to her in his bedroom. "He asks the right questions."

"He knows how to get me to think."

"I think he's right. I think you've changed a little."

"I know," Jason admitted. "It would be foolish for me to think Adderall, acid, and weed haven't changed me after seeing how Xanax changed you."

"Well, have I seemed normal lately?"

Jason nodded. "You've been great lately."

"Good. What were you hoping to get from Luke for tonight?"

"I don't know. Nothing in particular. I'm just upset about Chris, and I don't feel like socializing."

"Then why did you invite Jon and Bryan over?"

"I just want to keep them close. You can invite Jeff and Lisa over if you want. It's not like Chris is going to show up. The more people here, the less entertaining I'll have to do."

"Okay. Give me your phone. I'll call Lisa."

"Here," Jason said and handed over his iPhone. "I'll be right back." He left the room and headed to Luke's bedroom. He found Luke and Missy sitting on top of Luke's bed, watching TV.

"What's up?" Luke asked and raised his eyebrows at Jason.

"I forgot Chris gave me money Wednesday night to give you for weed. He wants fifty bucks worth," Jason said and reached into his pocket to retrieve the cash.

"I thought you said he wasn't coming tonight," Luke remarked.

"I'll give it to Jon to give to him," Jason said. "He'll see Chris before I will."

Luke climbed off his bed and headed over to his closet. "Do you want anything while I'm in my safe?" he asked.

Jason sighed. "What would get me in the mood to socialize?"

"Why aren't you in the mood to socialize?" Luke questioned him. "You're always up for that."

"I just have a lot on my mind," Jason replied vaguely.

"You should just snort a few lines of Adderall," Luke suggested. "That will get you going."

Jason rolled his eyes. "I hate Adderall. It's ruining my ability to sleep."

"Well, Vicodin, Xanax, and Klonopin are downers, so they're not going to put you in the mood to party," Luke stated matter-of-factly. "Unless you drink on Vicodin."

"Isn't that dangerous?" Jason asked.

Luke shrugged. "It's dangerous if you have more than one drink."

"Chris did that the night he almost overdosed," Jason recalled. "That kind of scared the crap out of me."

"Well, Chris also took Xanax, which was the main problem," Luke stated. "Mixing benzos and alcohol is always a bad idea."

"I don't know…I'll bounce the idea off Cathy. She'll probably get freaked out," Jason said. "The last time you gave her a PK, she puked for hours."

"Here," Luke said and tossed Jason a bag of weed—it was much larger than what fifty dollars typically bought. "Tell Chris he gets 'the family discount.'"

"O-kay," Jason said gradually, unsure of what Luke meant.

"Take a few of these in case you want them," Luke added and handed Jason three Vicodin. "Don't let Cathy take more than one."

Hesitantly, Jason took the pills from his brother. The idea of taking a painkiller freaked him out because of Chris's history with them. However, he was experiencing more emotional pain than he was used to, so the idea of relieving it was tempting.

"Oh, Jay," Missy called before jumping off the bed and going over to her pocketbook on the floor. "Cathy said some of her friends wanted cigarettes."

"She did?" Jason asked, wondering who planned on smoking and why Cathy would ever support that.

"Yeah, so I bought an extra pack," Missy replied and handed it to Jason.

"Do you smoke?" he asked, surprised that Missy even had cigarettes.

"Not unless I'm fall-down drunk!" Missy exclaimed. "I was buying them for some of my friends who aren't eighteen yet."

"I have no idea who Cathy wanted these for, but I'll let her know," Jason stated apprehensively. After he walked back to his bedroom, he threw the pack at Cathy.

"Where did these come from?!" she cried as she caught the pack with two hands.

"Missy said you asked her for them," Jason replied and raised his eyebrows at her.

Cathy looked confused. "I don't remember doing that," she admitted, "but I think I was kind of drunk at Chris's party."

"She said your friends wanted them," Jason clarified, "not you."

"Well, obviously," Cathy said. "I'm just surprised I asked her. I don't want my friends to smoke. I got mad at Lisa, Alyssa, and Leslie for trying it."

Jason shrugged. "Well, I'm sure someone at the party will take them if we just leave them on the counter. Do you think it was Lisa who asked for them?"

"I have no idea," Cathy replied. "It could have been Chris."

"Yeah, I guess. He said he's trying to quit, though."

"He says a lot of things," Cathy remarked.

"Should I call him?" Jason asked.

"About the cigarettes?"

"No!" Jason exclaimed. "About what happened today. I don't like things being weird between us."

"He asked for space, Jay," Cathy said matter-of-factly. "Calling him wouldn't be respecting that."

Jason sighed. "You're right."

"I hate seeing you so broken up over this. I know it sucks. Believe me—I know. Chantal was my best friend for my entire life until she stopped talking to me. You and Chris are like brothers. At least Chris said he wants the break to be temporary. I really don't think it's anything personal."

"I guess I'll know when I see how he treats everyone else."

"Jon and Bryan will be here soon. You have to cheer up."

Jason put his head down. "I'll tell them what happened. I'm sure they're wondering why Chris isn't coming tonight. What did Lisa say?"

"She said she'll come over after dinner with Leslie and Jeff."

"Okay, good. In the meantime, I have a proposition for you," Jason said with slight hesitation.

Cathy raised her eyebrows at him expectantly.

Jason took a deep breath. "I was just talking to Luke, and I told him I wasn't in the mood to party. He suggested I drink on Vicodin."

Cathy widened her green eyes. "Why would you do that?!"

"Well, it's a painkiller, so it might lighten my mood," Jason replied.

"Won't that just make you get drunk faster? You're kind of a jerk when you're drunk."

Jason sighed. "If you don't want me to do it, I won't."

"Why can't you just drink? Luke has beer and liquor. I'm sure he'll give you whatever you want. That should lighten your mood."

"Fine. I'll give the pills back and ask if we can make a few drinks," Jason said while glancing at the Vicodin in his hand.

"Good idea," Cathy stated flatly. She seemed disturbed that he was even entertaining the idea of taking a painkiller. He knew they were addictive, but Chris had never gotten addicted to them, and he had taken them on plenty of occasions.

"Well, I just thought of something else that could cheer me up!" Jason cried a few seconds later.

"Shooting heroin?" Cathy asked sarcastically.

Jason glared at her playfully. "Oh, shut up," he said and put the Vicodin down on his desk. He walked over to Cathy and lifted her off her feet. Seconds later, he tossed her onto his bed. "Who needs painkillers when I can hook up with you?"

Cathy widened her eyes, appearing startled. Jason found it strange but brushed it off. He shut and locked his door before joining Cathy on his bed.

"Jay, we can't," she said quietly. "I have my period."

"Ugh," Jason muttered. "Figures."

"Well, it's a good thing," Cathy remarked. "If I didn't, I'd be worried."

"Right... okay, so... Bryan and Jon will be here in a half hour. Want to just cuddle?"

Cathy looked at him sympathetically and then wrapped her arms around him. "I'm sorry you're so sad. Just don't let it drive you to do things that will put even more space between you and Chris."

Jason hugged her, realizing that she was speaking from experience. "I think he would approve of me cuddling with you," he responded facetiously.

Cathy and Jason lay in bed until Bryan called to say he and Jon had arrived. When Jason stood up to get the door, he decided to put the Vicodin in his Tylenol bottle so neither Bryan nor Jon would see it. Once Jon and Bryan were sitting in Jason's room, he began telling them about his conversation with Chris that morning.

Mid-story, Jon interrupted Jason to ask, "He was tripping the other night?"

"Oh... I probably shouldn't have told you that," Jason said, shoving his foot in his mouth. "I thought you knew."

Jon raised his eyebrows at Jason in surprise. "I assumed he drank and smoked weed. I didn't think he would ever take acid."

"Well, he got drunk and made a bad decision, and that's why he's all freaked out and not coming tonight," Jason said. He had completely forgotten that Jon and Bryan knew very little about Chris's drug use.

"Where did he even get acid?!" Bryan asked, looking as confused as Jon.

"Luke," Cathy spoke up, likely trying to come to Jason's rescue. "He has a connection. We don't know anything about it, though."

"Wow. I thought Chris was doing better," Jon commented. "He seemed really clear whenever we hung out lately. I thought—no offense, Bryan—that Courtney was really making a difference in his life."

Bryan let out a heavy breath. "She was, and that's why I don't hate him for going out with her."

"Do you hate *her*?" Cathy asked curiously.

Bryan shook his head. "No. I think she got mad at me for keeping her away from you guys for so long. I shouldn't have done that."

"Alyssa thinks she still likes you," Cathy said, trying to get a read on Bryan's feelings. "I think she probably does, too."

"She called me yesterday," Bryan admitted.

"Really, dude?" Jason questioned him. "Why?"

"Her parents bought her a cell phone, and she knew my number by heart," he replied with a shrug. "We only talked for a minute, but it was good to hear from her."

"Can we get back to the Chris-thing?" Jon asked in a disturbed tone while glancing from Bryan to Jason. "Why hasn't he said anything to us?"

"Probably because he doesn't want you to know he took acid," Jason reasoned. "I never should have told you."

"I'm not going to tell him I know," Jon promised, "but he's my best friend, and I'd like to know what's going on with him."

"All I can say is that he's mad at himself, and he's serious about getting sober," Jason responded matter-of-factly. "I'm upset that he feels the need to stay away for a while, but I can understand why he doesn't want to come tonight. There's going to be plenty of drugs and alcohol here. Luke is running the party, and he has the hookup."

"Is Luke who you get weed from?" Bryan asked.

Jason nodded.

"That makes sense. For some reason I always assumed Chris got it from Taylor," Bryan admitted.

Jason lowered his eyebrows. "Taylor hates it when Chris smokes."

"At a party two years ago, Taylor's friends told a story about Taylor giving kids coke so they could sober up for a beer pong tournament," Bryan recounted.

"Taylor?!" Jason cried. As far as he knew, Taylor had a good head on his shoulders. "Are you sure it wasn't Jordan?" he asked, believing that Jordan was wilder than his older brother.

"Chris told me Jordan doesn't touch drugs beyond weed," Bryan replied.

"Well, that could be true," Jason gathered. "He's doing really well at

ND."

"Chris also caught Taylor doing coke at a party," Bryan added. "Taylor's *not* the role model he led everyone to believe he was."

"Why hasn't Chris told me this?" Jason asked, shocked that Bryan knew more about Chris's family than he did.

"I only know because I was there," Bryan replied. "You were skiing at Sugarloaf with your family. Chris doesn't talk bad about people, so I'm sure that's why he didn't mention it."

"Holy $%&#!" Jason exclaimed. "I had no idea."

"Well, it makes more sense that Chris buys weed from Luke than from Taylor," Bryan said. "Taylor's never in Montgomery anymore."

"Oh, I almost forgot! Luke gave me this for Chris," Jason said and held up the bag of weed. "Jon, you'll see him before I do. Can you give it to him?"

Jon rolled his brown eyes. "Do I have to?"

Jason flipped his hands over. "Well, he's not going to talk to me. You're the straightedge one. If he's going to stay friends with anyone, it's you."

Jon sighed. "Fine but seal it tight. If my mom smells it when I go home, she'll kill me."

"It's not in a Ziploc bag," Jason said while eyeing the plastic bag precariously.

"Here," Cathy said and pulled a red ribbon off her wrist. "Tie it with this. I had it around my wrist to show what team I was on in gym. I forgot to take it off."

"Thanks," Jason said and took the ribbon from her. He tied the bag tightly and then tossed it at Jon. Considering the information that Bryan had shared and the fact that Taylor bought alcohol for Luke, Jason began to wonder if Taylor was Luke's connection. *Perhaps that was what Luke meant by "the family discount."*

CHAPTER 20

THROUGHOUT THE AFTERNOON, CATHY'S concern for Jason continued to increase. For months, he had been adamant about helping Chris stay away from painkillers, so to see him consider taking Vicodin showed Cathy how *off* he truly was.

Luke ended up offering Jason a bottle of vodka to drink with Cathy, Bryan, Leslie, and Jeff during their pregame—Jon and Lisa drank water, per usual. The alcohol seemed to lighten Jason's mood, but Cathy thought talking to his friends about the situation did even more for him. She was surprised that neither Jon nor Bryan had questioned why Chris felt the need to stay away from Jason specifically. As far as she knew, they had no idea that Jason had tried any recreational drugs beyond weed or alcohol.

Lisa was particularly interested in hearing about the situation with Chris. Cathy assumed she was happy that Chris was serious about getting sober. Jeff looked uncomfortable every time Lisa asked a question about Chris, and Cathy hoped it would not cause a problem between them because she really liked Jeff. Despite how close Lisa and Jeff had grown, Cathy feared Chris still owned her heart.

In an attempt to further lighten the mood, Jason packed a bowl and passed it around the room. To Cathy's surprise, Jeff took a hit. *How did Lisa manipulate you into that?* she thought as she watched Jeff pass the bowl to Leslie. After Leslie took a hit, she offered it to Jon, who strongly declined. Cathy assumed Jon felt a bit out of place because everyone else was high, buzzed, or both.

"What time are Alyssa and Courtney coming?" Cathy questioned him, thinking if she could drag him into the conversation, then he might feel a bit more comfortable.

"I think around eight," Jon replied.

"Ooooh! Bry-guy!" Jason sang in a taunting manner. "Are you excited to see Courtney?"

Bryan rolled his eyes. "Stop."

Cathy shot daggers at Jason, hoping he would leave Bryan alone. Courtney was a sensitive topic for him and an awkward one for everyone else. Cathy *really* hoped Jason would not touch the Vicodin Luke gave him because he was already more buzzed than she liked. Alcohol, more often than not, turned her warmhearted boyfriend into the biggest A-hole she knew.

CHAPTER 21

By the time Alyssa and Courtney arrived at the party, Jason could not even walk straight. Cathy, on the other hand, had cut herself off after two drinks. She was planning to sleep over Alyssa's that night, and she couldn't go there noticeably buzzed because Alyssa's parents were incredibly perceptive and strict.

"Hi, guys!" Courtney exclaimed vibrantly as Jason led her and Alyssa into the kitchen where Cathy, Jon, Lisa, Jeff, and Leslie were gathered.

"Hey, Court!" Jon cried in a friendly tone. "Where's your man?"

Courtney shrugged. "I guess he's not coming out tonight. Is Bryan here?" she asked.

"Well, you see Court-ney," Jason sang, placing his arm around her shoulders. "I had some herb and a pipe. Jon, Bry-guy, and a few others came over after school, so we pregamed up in my room. Some of my guests have brought more weed, but my pipe and papers are upstairs."

"So, Bryan went up to get them?" Courtney asked and gazed at him questioningly.

Jason nodded. "Do you want something to drink?" he offered while holding up a bottle of vodka.

"Uh, not right now," Courtney replied, edging herself away from Jason. "Not ever," she added quietly.

At that moment, it became apparent to Cathy how out-of-place Courtney felt. If she was straightedge and her boyfriend was trying to become straightedge, then why was she at the party? "Seeing that Chris isn't coming, I'm surprised you came," Cathy remarked.

"Why?" Courtney questioned her in a confused manner.

"Hey!" Bryan exclaimed as he and Courtney collided. "Court, what's up?"

Courtney immediately embraced him.

"What was that for?" Bryan asked while handing the pipe and papers to Jason.

"Who wants a hit?" Jason sang as soon as he began rolling a joint.

"You know I'm all set with that crap," Bryan responded while grabbing Courtney's hand and pulling her closer into his arms.

Cathy widened her eyes as she watched Courtney allow Bryan to pull her body into his. As shy as Bryan was, Cathy had to give him credit for going after his girl. As Cathy made her way over to Jason, she deliberately bumped Courtney further into Bryan—just to let her know she had noticed their flirting. As she waited for Jason to finish rolling the joint, she watched Courtney and Bryan interact.

"Did Jay offer you a drink?" Bryan questioned her, reaching into the nearly empty thirty-rack on the counter.

"Yeah, he did," Courtney replied, "but please don't drink tonight, Bry." She placed her left hand onto Bryan's arm and looked pleadingly into his eyes.

"All right," Bryan agreed with ease. "What's going on?"

Courtney sighed and placed her head on Bryan's shoulder.

"Court, what's wrong?" Bryan asked, lifting her chin and searching her eyes.

Courtney remained silent.

"What?" Bryan pressed, gently brushing a piece of jet-black hair from her flushed face.

"Do you think we could go somewhere and talk?" Courtney asked.

"Absolutely," Bryan said with a nod. "Hey, Jay?"

"Hey, what's up?" Jason replied, without glancing in Bryan's direction.

Bryan walked over to him with Courtney close behind him. "Can, uh, we go talk in your room?" he whispered.

Jason laughed loudly and glanced from Bryan to Courtney.

Oh, God, Cathy thought. *I can't wait for the rude comment that's sure to come next!*

"Yeah, dude. Help yourself! There are some condoms in the nightstand if you need one!" Jason exclaimed.

Courtney dropped her jaw and widened her eyes in horror. Cathy was quite certain her expression mirrored Courtney's as she glared at her boyfriend in disbelief. *You are such an idiot,* she thought. *Now, people are going to assume we had sex!*

"Oh, shut up," Bryan snapped, pushing Jason hard in the shoulder.

Laughter erupted from their friends' mouths, and numerous pairs of eyes darted from Courtney to Bryan.

"Yay!" Alyssa clapped, sending a mischievous smirk in Courtney's direction.

Courtney blushed deeply and followed Bryan out of the kitchen with her head down.

As soon as Courtney and Bryan were out of hearing distance, Cathy turned toward Jason. "Leave them alone!" she cried and slapped his arm. "Bryan deserves every chance to get her back."

Jason laughed. "I one hundred percent agree!" he exclaimed. "%&#$ Chris!"

Cathy widened her eyes in awe of what Jason had just said.

"Don't say that, guy," Jon said, eyeing Jason uneasily. "You two had a little fight, but it'll blow over. He's still our best friend."

"He's still *your* best friend," Jason stated matter-of-factly. "My best friend doesn't turn his back on me. That's all I'm saying."

Cathy rolled her eyes before locking them on Jon. "He's just drunk," she mouthed silently to him and then shook her head disapprovingly.

"I need some air," Jon said and turned abruptly away from Jason. He walked across the kitchen and stepped onto the back porch without saying a word to anyone.

"You really pissed off Jon," Lisa remarked.

"Who cares," Jason said while passing her the joint.

"I don't think I want this," Lisa commented and handed it to Cathy. "I'm still pretty high from earlier. How are you guys not totally baked?"

"I think I am," Cathy replied and handed the joint back to her boyfriend without taking a hit.

"Whose thirty-rack is that on the counter?" Alyssa asked.

"One of Luke's friends brought it," Jason answered. "Help yourself."

"Won't Jon get mad if you drink?" Leslie asked.

"He's already mad," Alyssa responded and reached for a can of beer.

"Yeah, at Jay—not you," Leslie stated matter-of-factly.

Alyssa shrugged carelessly and cracked open the beer.

"Are you two in a fight?" Lisa asked.

"He walks all over me," Alyssa replied. "He thinks he owns me because I slept with him. I need to show him that he doesn't."

Cathy and Leslie widened their eyes.

"You slept with him?!" Lisa cried after dropping her jaw.

"Yup," Alyssa stated flatly.

"Okay... girl talk... JB, let's go somewhere else," Jason commented and nodded for Jeff to follow him out of the kitchen.

Cathy felt a significant amount of relief after Jason left the room. Despite how high she was, her boyfriend's attitude was giving her anxiety.

"When?!" Lisa exclaimed.

Alyssa sighed. "Last month," she admitted. "We almost did it in July, but I wasn't ready, so we waited until August, but... I still don't think I was ready."

Cathy was relieved to hear she wasn't the only non-virgin among her girlfriends, but she felt bad for Alyssa. She knew what it was like to regret giving up your virginity. It had given Jason some sort of power over her, which sounded exactly like what Alyssa was describing. Cathy had been withholding sex from Jason since their second time, always having an excuse up her sleeve, but pretty soon she was going to run out of excuses and have to tell him the truth. She dreaded that conversation immensely.

"Did you tell anyone?" Leslie asked.

Alyssa shook her head. "No, but Jon told Chris and Bryan."

"Well, they don't have big mouths," Lisa said, "but now Jay knows, so watch out!"

Alyssa rolled her eyes. "He would have found out soon enough, anyway."

"Jay won't say anything in sobriety," Cathy assured her.

"I thought if we had sex it would bring us closer," Alyssa admitted, "but all it did was make me feel less secure about our relationship. In the back of my mind, I'm pretty sure he still loves Chantal. I thought sleeping with him would change that, but it didn't. Now she's what he's never had, and I'm disposable."

"Lyss, you guys have been best friends for years. You are not disposable," Leslie commented matter-of-factly. "Why do you think he still loves Chantal? She's been with Andy for, like, a year."

Alyssa shrugged. "I stood by his side through their breakup. I saw how much it hurt him. I know what he's like when he's filled with emotion. He's not like that with me."

"Well, maybe that's good," Lisa suggested. "After all, they're not together anymore, so maybe being filled with emotion isn't the best thing for a relationship."

Cathy assumed Lisa was speaking from personal experience. Her relationship with Chris had been very emotional, whereas her relationship with Jeff seemed strategic.

"Lis, you know what I'm talking about," Alyssa said and looked her straight in the eye, "because you're Jon, and Chris is Chantal."

"I'm over Chris," Lisa stated defensively.

"I would like to believe that because Chris has been acting really weird lately, but I don't," Alyssa retorted.

"My breakup with Chris was *nothing* like Chantal and Jon's breakup," Lisa stressed. "Chris and I broke up in hopes that he could straighten out his life. Chantal and Jon broke up over…well…whatever they broke up over…" As Lisa swallowed her words, Cathy felt guilty about Chantal and Jon's breakup for the first time in a long time. Chantal and Jon broke up over "nothing" is what Lisa had most likely been about to say. Sixteen months later, Cathy was certain Jon still loved her twin.

"Over what?" Alyssa asked. "Don't even say over me!"

"I wasn't going to say that," Lisa said. "They broke up because he was being a jerk to her. He was walking all over her. She became a doormat to him, and they never even had sex once! I think what you're experiencing is just Jon being himself. He did the same thing to Chantal. Once he had her heart, he trampled on it. Maybe he didn't know he had yours until you slept with him. I don't know what made him realize he had Chantal's, but he messed with her head, too."

"It was when she covered for him after he got high," Cathy spoke up. "She chose to protect him over being open with my parents."

"That's a good point," Lisa said. "After that he started spending all of his time with you, Lyss."

"No. Jon came to me to sort out his personal issues. He didn't hit on me. He didn't talk bad about Chantal. He was trying to find himself after he lost himself by engaging in Chris's behavior," Alyssa stated firmly. "I was there. I know what happened. You guys have all rewritten the story of Jon and Chantal's breakup so many times that you have no idea what's true or false. But I *know* he was trying to better himself for her. He loved her. He *still* loves her, and I'm still his shoulder to cry on—his wet blanket." With that, she turned and walked out of the kitchen.

"Yikes," Lisa said and widened her eyes. "He's in her head."

"I still don't get their breakup," Leslie admitted. "Neither Chantal nor Jon is a liar. They both claim they got dumped. It makes no sense at all."

Lisa shot her eyes at Cathy, looking alarmed. "Why don't we go find the boys?" she suggested, clearly trying to change the subject.

"I'm going to check on Lyss," Cathy replied. "I bet Jay and Jeff are somewhere with Jon."

"All right. Come find us after," Lisa said and nodded for Leslie to follow her.

A moment later, Cathy found Alyssa sitting by herself in the formal living room located off the foyer. "Hey," she greeted her quietly. "Do you want to leave?"

"No. I just need to calm down before I hang out with everyone," Alyssa replied. "I'll be fine. Just give me a few minutes."

"Okay," Cathy agreed and turned back into the foyer. She glanced up the stairs, wondering what Courtney and Bryan were doing in Jason's room. If they were to get back together, that would surely shake up their group.

CHAPTER 22

TEN MINUTES LATER, CATHY was outside on Jason's deck with her friends when Alyssa came up behind Jon and affectionately wrapped her arms around him. "Hi, handsome," she greeted him cheerfully.

"Hey," Jon responded. "Where've you been?"

"Just inside," she replied vaguely and then released him from her arms. Jon put his arm around her shoulders and pulled her into the circle in which everyone was standing. They had been casually discussing the first two days of school: their classes, classmates, and teachers. Only Jason, Jeff, and Leslie were drinking. Despite the rowdy party occurring around them, their close friends were having a pretty chill night...until Andy showed up.

"Andy?" Lisa cried out when she spotted her best friend. "I can't believe you're here!"

Cathy immediately shot her eyes at Jon, wondering if the sight of Andy would still bother him. Jon looked nauseated.

"Hey!" Andy greeted Lisa warmly. He slapped Jeff's hand before leaning in to hug Lisa and Leslie. "What's up, guys?" he said casually to everyone else. He was dressed neatly in khaki shorts and a plaid, button-up shirt. Cathy was surprised he would "stoop to the level" of hanging out with her group of friends. Thankfully, Cathy did not have a drink in her hand, for she would have felt further judged. She began to wonder what Chantal was up to and why Andy wasn't with her.

"Welcome!" Jason greeted Andy and patted him on the shoulder. "Did you come with Robby?"

Andy nodded. "Yeah, he wanted to check on Katie. They're back together. I don't think we're staying too long."

"Do you want anything to drink?" Jason asked.

"What do you have?" Andy responded.

"There's soda, water, beer, vodka—a whole bunch of options inside," Jason replied. "Follow me," he added.

Cathy trailed behind them, unable to keep her curiosity at bay. She wondered if Andy was still straightedge. He had partied at the beginning of seventh grade until he lost Chantal to Jon. He had been strait-laced, supposedly, ever since. According to Lisa, Andy did not drink or smoke, but then again, Lisa could have meant he did not drink or smoke "every day." Lately, she had heard a lot of people—Luke, Lisa, Jason—say that they did not "do" certain things, even though they technically did. Cathy could not help but wonder how many times someone would have to "do" something to consider themselves a "doer" of it.

"Water's good," Andy said after Jason opened the refrigerator.

"Do you want vodka-spiked water?" Jason asked and raised his eyebrows. "Robby will never know the difference."

Andy laughed and looked at Cathy. "I'm all set."

"Oh, don't worry about Cathy telling Chantal," Jason said and waved him off. "Chantal wouldn't talk to her if their house was burning down."

Cathy and Andy both widened their eyes.

"What?" Jason asked and glanced back and forth between them. "Did I not just say something *wicked obvious*?"

"Ugh, Jay, you're drunk," Cathy whined and playfully wrapped her arm around his shoulders. "Leave Andy alone."

"Are you going to drink?" Andy questioned Cathy.

Cathy shook her head from side to side.

"I'm good with water but thanks anyway, Jay," Andy said assuredly.

"No problem," Jason remarked and retrieved a bottle of water for Andy.

"Jay! Can you make me another drink?" Leslie called as she came running into the kitchen with Alyssa. "And get Alyssa a beer?"

"You're going to drink in front of Jon?" Jason questioned Alyssa. "He'll kick your ass."

Alyssa rolled her hazel eyes. "I don't care; he's done worse."

"Touché," Jason sang. "There should still be beer left in one of the beer balls. Leslie, vodka and Sprite?"

Leslie nodded.

"When did *you* start drinking?" Andy questioned Leslie, eyeing her strangely.

"A lot later in life than *you*," Leslie retorted with a flirtatious sparkle in her green eyes.

"Yeah, I got some things out of my system early," Andy admitted with an uncomfortable laugh. "Does Lisa drink, too?"

Leslie shook her head. "Not anymore—not since her dad's accident."

"That's what she told me," Andy said, "but with her you never really know," he added.

"Did she tell you she doesn't smoke, too?" Cathy wondered out loud. "Because that's what she told me!"

"Smoking is her pet peeve," Andy stated matter-of-factly. "She berated me for trying it."

Cathy raised her eyebrows at Andy. "Right. I know, but she's been acting a little weird lately."

Andy lowered his eyebrows, looking perplexed. "I'll talk to her," he resounded. Despite Cathy's belief that Andy was a snob, like the majority of his friends, he was being warm and friendly to everyone.

Seconds later, Alyssa appeared beside them with a cup of foamy beer. "Well, I better get this over with," she said and took a deep breath. "Brace yourself for the eruption that is Jon's temper."

"Can't wait," Jason muttered and motioned for everyone to follow Alyssa back outside. Although it was ten o'clock, it was still over seventy degrees out. A lot of people were on the deck; some were even swimming in the pool.

Cathy was surprised that Alyssa would deliberately upset Jon. Then again, she assumed Alyssa's goal was to decipher where Jon's true feelings lay. If he didn't love her, then he wouldn't put up with behavior he considered "beneath" his standards; if he didn't love her, then she deserved to know. In seventh grade, Jon had expected Chantal to be patient with him while he experimented with alcohol and weed. Alyssa likely felt that Jon—in the name of love—should extend her the same courtesy. However, Cathy knew that was not how Jon's mind worked. He was an emotional being with a short fuse and lofty principles.

CHAPTER 23

L ESS THAN AN HOUR later, the chant of the party fell silent as Jon indignantly stomped into the kitchen, screaming Alyssa's name. *Saw this coming,* Cathy thought as she locked her eyes on him. Although Andy had left a half hour prior, Jon had remained agitated. Cathy assumed he was furious that Alyssa had not only drunk a couple of beers, but also taken a haul off someone's cigarette and later a hit off a joint. Alyssa was clearly in full-on rebellion mode because, as far as Cathy knew, she had never smoked weed in her life. Afterward, Jon had left the kitchen and gone upstairs with Courtney and Bryan, who had only momentarily joined the party.

"What the heck is your problem?" Jon cried as he came up behind his girlfriend.

"Jon?" Alyssa asked as she turned around in confusion.

"Yeah, it's your boyfriend, letting you know you're an embarrassment!" Jon exclaimed.

Alyssa stared at him blankly.

"I've had it!" Jon continued, drawing more attention their way.

"Jon, what is wrong with you?" Alyssa questioned him quietly.

"We're through," Jon stated flatly, looking eye-to-eye with her. "You've changed into someone I could never have a steady relationship with. I feel like I don't even know who you are. To this day, Chantal means more to me than you ever could."

Ouch. Cathy winced. *Oh, Jon. Did you really have to go there? You are the king of breaking hearts.*

A single tear streaked from Alyssa's right eye as she stared at Jon in awe of what was happening. Her pain likely stemmed most deeply from the realization that her gut instinct had been right: Jon did care more about Chantal than her.

When Alyssa glanced at Cathy, Cathy dropped her eyes to the floor. She had to do everything in her power to stop herself from attacking Jon. For what he had done to Chantal and for what he was doing to Alyssa, Cathy officially hated him. She wondered if Jason would step in and do something—perhaps pull Jon aside and tell him to chill out. Nothing but a short laugh escaped from Jason's mouth, and Cathy realized he was far too wasted to stand up for Alyssa. If he wasn't going to, then Cathy would have to. At that moment, she missed Chris, who would have come to Alyssa's defense without a second thought.

"Alyssa!" Courtney suddenly cried, stepping out from behind Bryan and moving between Alyssa and Jon.

Cathy darted her eyes at Courtney, surprised she had the gall to say anything.

Alyssa gazed helplessly at Courtney as Luke came rushing into the room. "%$&^! The cops are here!" he announced frantically.

"Crap!" Jason exclaimed, turning his attention to the more serious dilemma. "Everyone, get out of my house!"

All eyes were torn off Alyssa, Courtney, and Jon as chaos erupted throughout the house. The pounding on the front door was barely heard over the uproar of people scrambling towards alternative exits. Alyssa immediately burst into tears and fell to the floor as her friends ran away from her.

"Cathy! To the pool house! Now!" Jason cried, tugging on her arm.

"Alyssa, we have to go!" Cathy exclaimed, dropping to the ground beside her. "We need to get out of here."

Alyssa said nothing. She merely continued sobbing hysterically.

"Cathy! Now!" Jason repeated.

"Go! Just go!" Cathy yelled to her boyfriend before turning back to Alyssa. "Lyss, come on. We have to get out of here."

"I told you he loved her," Alyssa stated and looked up helplessly at Cathy. Her eyes were full of pain—deep pain—which made Cathy's eyes also fill with tears.

"He's just mad, Lyss," Cathy remarked. "We need to find somewhere to hide right now."

Alyssa seemed to suddenly snap out of her daze and realize the urgency of the situation. "What do we do?!" she asked frantically and stood up.

Cathy jumped up beside her as multiple police officers entered the kitchen. She widened her eyes, realizing they were out of options. "We cry," she whispered to Alyssa. "Cry your eyes out! Your boyfriend just dumped you." She hugged Alyssa tightly. "Cry as hard as you can," she added before beginning to sob as well. With the cops surrounding them, they would need to draw all the sympathy they could get.

CHAPTER 24

Two hours later, Cathy walked into her house with her parents, feeling extremely frustrated. Even though she and Alyssa had not been drunk, the cops had put them, along with ten to fifteen other teens from the party, into a paddy wagon and brought them to the police station. The police officers did not even ask Alyssa or Cathy to take a sobriety test because they appeared sober. Although neither of them had been charged with anything, their parents were furious. On the drive home from the police station, neither Cathy's mother nor father had spoken a word to her.

"Okay, so what? Am I grounded?" Cathy questioned her parents as they entered the kitchen, hoping one of them would say *something*.

"Boy, is that an understatement!" her father laughed.

"Cathaleen, what made you do this?" her mother asked, staring at her in awe. She sat down at the kitchen table and eyed Cathy in a concerned manner.

"Do what, Mom?" Cathy responded in annoyance. "Do I suddenly not measure up to Chantal? Am I not the perfect little angel I've led you to believe I am?" She could not believe her parents were upset with her for being at her own boyfriend's house!

"Cathy, we just want to know what has influenced you," her father pressed. "Whether you see it as wrong or not, getting arrested is not going to please us. Not to mention that you lied and said you were sleeping at Alyssa's."

"I would have slept at Alyssa's after the party if the cops hadn't shown up," Cathy replied. "So, don't even say I lied!"

"You never mentioned a party to us," her mother stated.

"Oh, so it would have been okay if I had 'mentioned' the party?" Cathy asked. "You know how out of control Jason's brothers can get. You wouldn't have let me go to the party if I had asked you for permission. Jason's my boyfriend. I had to be there."

Her mother sighed. "You can deal with her, Michael. I'm going to bed. I never thought she and Chantal could grow so far apart," she said as she rose from the table.

"Mom, I didn't do anything wrong," Cathy whined, trailing behind her mother into the hallway.

"Enough," her mother snapped. "We will talk more about this tomorrow."

"Dad!" Cathy cried and turned back into the kitchen. "I didn't do anything wrong. I could have hidden from the cops like my other friends did, but Alyssa and I stayed in plain sight. We didn't have anything to hide. We weren't drunk! I didn't think they could bring me to the police station just for being at Jason's house."

Mr. Kagelli took a deep breath. "Cathy, I believe you're naïve enough not to expect to get in trouble for being at a party, but that doesn't excuse what you were a part of tonight. We were told that there was not only alcohol, but also marijuana there. Why would you willingly surround yourself with such sinful vices?"

Cathy cocked her head to the side, realizing her father believed her. "I'm sorry, Dad," she said, conjuring up a tone of remorse. "I just wanted to spend time with Jason. I realize now that we shouldn't hang out with the older kids."

"Well, I don't think you'll be hanging out with anyone for quite some time," her father remarked, "and I doubt your boyfriend will be either."

"Jason had nothing to do with the party," Cathy said. "I bet he won't even get grounded."

Mr. Kagelli sighed. "It pains me to do it, but you need to be disciplined. You are a Christian who is supposed to represent the light in a dark world, not partake in it."

"Did you ever go to a party in high school?" Cathy asked.

"Of course," her father replied, "but not during the first week."

Cathy rolled her eyes.

"I'll talk to your mother, and we will figure out an appropriate punishment for you. I respect that you did not run from the police, but if you want us to trust you, then you need to be more open with us. Your mother would not be so upset if she had known you were going to be at Jason's. She thought you were at Alyssa's, so the phone call we got from the police station came as a complete shock."

"I'm sorry," Cathy said and hung her head. "I went to Jason's after school, and Alyssa's brother was supposed to pick us up at eleven."

"One of the police officers mentioned that you and Alyssa were crying," her father remarked. "Was that just because you were scared?"

"No," Cathy replied and shook her head. "Jon broke up with Alyssa right before the cops showed up. He told her he cared more about Chantal, actually."

Mr. Kagelli lowered his eyebrows.

"I was crying because I felt bad for her," Cathy added. "Jon was meaner than he needed to be. She didn't deserve to get yelled at in front of everyone at the party."

"So, he breaks Chantal's heart, goes after Alyssa, and then breaks up with Alyssa because he still has feelings for Chantal?" her father asked in a perplexed manner.

"Something like that," Cathy replied uncomfortably.

"That boy makes no sense," her father said. "It's sad that he no longer attends church. He's fallen by the wayside."

Cathy looked up at her dad. "The youth group kids were mean to him, so I don't blame him for not going, but he was definitely a nicer person when he went."

"I'm sure. Well, it's late," her father said and glanced at the nearby clock. "Why don't you go upstairs, get some sleep, and we'll talk more about things tomorrow."

"Where's Chantal?" Cathy asked as she turned to leave the kitchen.

"She's at Chris's house," her father replied.

Cathy's heartbeat stopped in its place. She whipped her head around to look at her dad, wondering if she had misheard him. "What?"

"Chris invited her to go pick up his girlfriend at—I'm guessing—the party you were at. He was afraid she was going to get it trouble for being there."

Nothing her father said made any sense. Courtney had been with Bryan at the party, and Chantal had not spoken to Chris in over a year. "Chantal's not friends with Chris anymore," Cathy stated in a confused manner.

Her father shrugged. "Well, she asked to go, and we let her. We assumed she would get a ride back here, but Chris's cousin dropped everyone off at

Chris's house. She called us for a ride home, but we had just gotten the call from the police, so we couldn't pick her up."

"So, she's still there?" Cathy questioned him in awe of what she was hearing.

Her father nodded. "We didn't know how long we would be tied up with you at the police station, so we agreed to let her stay. We trust her."

At that point, Cathy began to wonder if she was dreaming. As good at connecting the dots as she typically was, she could not think of any reason why Chris would invite Chantal to go with him to pick up Courtney. As far as she knew, Chantal did not even know Courtney.

CHAPTER 25

Cathy awoke around ten o'clock on Saturday morning, dreading the impending conversation with her parents. She had been unable to get ahold of Jason before falling asleep, so she awoke feeling incredibly curious to hear about the rest of his night. She opted to call him before talking to her parents, astutely fearing they would ground her from the phone.

"Hey!" Jason's voice rang into her ear thirty seconds later. "I'm sorry I missed your call last night. What happened to you? Are you okay?"

Cathy let out a heavy breath. "The cops brought me and Alyssa to the police station with Matt and some other kids. We didn't get charged with anything, but my parents are PISSED… like, seriously pissed… like I may be grounded for the next year *pissed*."

"Oh, man," Jason said, sounding disheartened. "I'm *so* sorry. Should I come over and apologize to them for getting you in trouble?"

"Maybe… I'm not sure… I'll let you know how it goes when I talk to them. I just woke up," Cathy replied.

"So, last night is kind of a blur," Jason admitted. "I'm sure I was a jerk and owe you an apology for something. Why didn't you hide in the pool house with me?"

Cathy took a deep breath. "Because Alyssa was in shock over what Jon said, and I couldn't get her to leave the kitchen."

"What happened between Alyssa and Jon?"

"You don't remember?"

"Told you—fuzzy."

Cathy sighed. "He broke up with her in the middle of the party and told her Chantal meant more to him than she did."

"What?!" Jason exclaimed. "Why?"

"He was upset that Andy showed up, and then Alyssa fueled the fire by drinking and smoking," Cathy explained. "Jon was a complete jerk. I officially hate him."

"So, he didn't get taken to the police station with you?"

"No. Who was in the pool house?"

"I'm pretty sure it was me, Luke, Missy, Lisa, Jeff, Leslie, and a handful of my brothers' friends. I can't believe they arrested Matt. My parents had to take the first ferry over from Nantucket this morning. They're not happy."

"Poor Matt!" Cathy cried. "It wasn't even his party."

"The cops drug-tested him, and he passed with flying colors, so my parents were relieved. They didn't charge him with anything, but they informed my parents that they found some weed in the house. We are having a family meeting this afternoon. I don't know what's going to happen. I could easily lie and say I wasn't home, but I don't want Matt to take all the heat. Luke should take the blame, and I can only make sure that happens if I tell my side of the story."

"They're not going to hold anything against *you*," Cathy assumed. "You had, like, five friends over, and you're the baby. You can't control what your brothers do."

"I know," Jason agreed. "But, wait. How much trouble are you in? Your mom must have flipped out! Did they drug-test you?"

"Thankfully no! They thought Alyssa and I seemed sober, so they didn't make us take any sobriety tests. We were both crying our eyes out, so I think they felt bad."

Jason let out a sigh of relief. "You lucked out. I wonder what happened to Courtney, Bryan, and Jon."

"Oh!" Cathy exclaimed. "This is weird! Last night, my dad told me Chantal went with Chris to pick up Courtney at your house."

"Huh?"

"Yeah… I can't make any sense of it. She ended up sleeping at Chris's house because my parents were busy dealing with the cops."

"What?!" Jason cried and let out a short laugh. "Nothing you're saying makes sense."

"I know!" Cathy cried. "Chantal doesn't associate with Chris or Courtney. You probably don't remember, but Courtney was up in your bedroom with

Bryan the whole night, so I don't know why she would have asked Chris to come get her. It wasn't because of the cops because Chantal was already with Chris when the police called my parents."

"I feel like we are living in Bizarro World right now," Jason stated. "See what you can find out from Chantal, and I'll try to get in touch with Bryan and Jon."

"Oh, Jon's pretty pissed at you," Cathy warned him.

"Why?" Jason asked. "What did I say?"

"You said 'eff Chris.'"

Jason groaned. "Oh, great. That's the last thing I need Chris hearing about right now."

"You shouldn't drink," Cathy stated matter-of-factly. "You turn into a jerk."

Jason sighed. "I'll keep that in mind."

"Well, let me know if you hear anything from Bryan or Jon. There's a good chance that I'll be grounded from the phone, but I have my iPad, so I can message you."

"Oh, good," Jason said. "I'm going to buy you a cell phone for Christmas."

"Let's just hope I'm allowed to use my house phone before then!" Cathy cried.

"I'm super curious about this Chantal and Chris thing," Jason admitted. "Let me know as soon as you find out more."

"That makes two of us! I would never have thought Andy would be at your house and Chantal would be at Chris's house."

"Did Andy come with his brother?"

"Yeah. They came to pick up Katie before it got too rowdy. They were long gone before the cops showed up."

"So, maybe he's not a snob?"

"I was actually thinking the same thing," Cathy admitted. "He was super friendly. Maybe it's just Chantal, Katherine, Bobby, and Adam who look down on us. Andy *is* Lisa's best friend, after all. I don't think he would have come if he had anything against us."

"Well, that's good to know. Maybe if he becomes friends with us, he'll get Chantal to talk to you."

"That would be amazing, but it's doubtful," Cathy commented, glancing at a picture on her nightstand from seventh grade of her and Chantal. "I'm done getting my hopes up about her."

"I don't blame you, but it's not a bad thing to have hope. If she hung out with Chris, then maybe she's starting to come around to our friends."

"Doubtful, but I'll let you know what I find out," Cathy said before hanging up the phone. She took a deep breath before leaving her bedroom and braced herself for the overly harsh punishment that was sure to come. As she began to walk past Chantal's bedroom an idea entered her mind.

Taking a deep breath, she stopped in her tracks. A moment later, she stepped up to Chantal's bedroom door and hesitated only slightly before knocking on it. A few seconds later, she heard movement from within the room.

When Chantal opened her door, she appeared startled to see Cathy. "What?" she asked with wide eyes.

"I think we should have a little chat about last night," Cathy replied and raised her eyebrows. "You'll be interested in what I have to say."

"Didn't you get thrown in jail?" Chantal questioned her.

Cathy rolled her eyes. "I was actually hanging out with your boyfriend before that happened."

"Yeah... So?"

"And your ex-boyfriend."

"I saw him last night, too," Chantal retorted and crossed her arms.

"Oh, did Jon go to Chris's house after the party?"

Chantal eyed Cathy warily and then sighed. "Just come in," she said and stepped aside to let Cathy into her messy bedroom.

CHAPTER 26

ATHY SPENT SOME TIME filling Chantal in on Jon and Andy's interactions at the party, as well as the drama that had taken place between Jon and Alyssa. She did not tell her what Alyssa had done to provoke Jon, but she hinted that everyone thought Jon still had feelings for Chantal.

Chantal appeared a bit shaken up by the news. "I really don't understand him," she admitted. "Why would he dump me for Alyssa if he still loved me? Our breakup makes no sense."

"You're right. That's why I never believed he dumped you for Alyssa," Cathy remarked. "She was dumb to go out with him. She's known all along that he still loves you."

Chantal eyed Cathy warily.

"How did you end up at Chris's house last night?" Cathy asked, hoping to change the subject before Chantal got too upset.

"Marc Dunkin and I picked up Jon, Courtney, and Bryan from Jason's after the cops left. I didn't really talk to Jon," Chantal replied. "We were supposed to pick up Courtney earlier, but the first time we went, the cops were in the driveway, so we left. I saw Jon again this morning. He was with a girl—not Alyssa."

"How did you end up with Marc and Chris?" Cathy asked. She had assumed Marc had been at the party, but now that she thought about it, she could not recall seeing him. "Do you know Courtney from school?"

Chantal shook her head. "No. Courtney's best friend Marielle—the girl who sits on the other side of me in homeroom—came over last night. We became friends this week. Chris called to see if I had heard from you. He was worried about Courtney getting in trouble at Jay's. I connected him with Marielle, and then Marielle got in touch with Courtney."

"Hmmm," Cathy said thoughtfully, trying to picture Marielle. "I thought you said you were only with Marc?"

Chantal bit her bottom lip. "Marielle and Chris waited at Chris's house so Courtney, Jon, and Bryan could fit in the truck."

"Why didn't Marc and Chris go get them?"

"Um…Chris broke up with Courtney last night," Chantal stated after a bit of hesitation.

Cathy widened her eyes. "Did she hook back up with Bryan?!"

Chantal shrugged. "I'm not quite sure."

Cathy lowered her eyebrows. "So, you went instead of Chris because things were awkward between him and Courtney?" Cathy gathered.

"Chris tried to cheat on Courtney with Marielle," Chantal said, taking Cathy by complete surprise.

Cathy widened her eyes. "With her best friend?!"

"Yeah. I guess she's in his biology class. According to him, he scoped her out on the first day of school, not knowing she was Courtney's friend. Marielle pushed him away, but he seemed pretty into her."

Cathy sat in disbelief of what she was hearing. "Has he lost his mind?" she wondered out loud. "I've never seen him act so all over the place."

"He seemed okay," Chantal replied with a shrug. "Chris has always been a big flirt."

"Yeah, but to make a move on her *best friend*? That's bold!" Cathy exclaimed.

"Isn't that what your friends do?" Chantal retorted.

Chantal had a point. If Courtney hadn't been morally off limits to Chris, then why would Courtney's best friend be off limits? "So, does Chris want to date Marielle?"

Chantal shrugged.

"Wait…who was the girl with Jon this morning?" Cathy questioned her curiously.

"Courtney's other friend, Julianna," Chantal replied.

"Blonde?" Cathy asked.

Chantal nodded.

"Julianna Camen?"

Chantal nodded again.

"I have a few classes with her. She seems super shy. How the heck did Jon end up with her?"

"Ask him," Chantal replied, sounding careless. "She seemed pretty upset. I guess Courtney was mean to her during the first couple of days of school. Marielle said Courtney ditched Julianna for your friends."

"We barely know Courtney. Why would she ditch her friend to hang out with us?"

Chantal crossed her arms and eyed Cathy in an amused manner. "C'mon, you know why."

Cathy sent her sister a puzzled look, wondering what she was implying. "Jason and I don't care who she's friends with. I don't think Chris would ever ask her to ditch her friends for his."

"What do you think of Courtney?" Chantal asked.

"I think she's a good influence on Chris, even though she ditched him for a party and probably hooked back up with Bryan."

"I think she wants to be popular," Chantal stated flatly. "Bryan kept her away from your friends for so long that she idolizes you guys. She ditched her best friends *and* Chris to attend Jason's party with Alyssa."

"High school just started!" Cathy cried. "How can anyone in our grade be 'popular' yet?"

"When there's a party at Jason's house, if you're cool, you're there," Chantal remarked.

Cathy was dumbfounded by everything her sister was saying. If what she said was true, then Jason's read on Courtney had been accurate.

"You realize that, right?" Chantal pressed, drawing Cathy away from her thoughts.

"That's just because of Matt and Luke," Cathy replied. "Matt's the captain of the football team, and Luke's the hottest guy at our school. They're popular. Jason's just forced into their shenanigans."

"How humble of you," Chantal remarked. "Do you really have no idea that nearly every girl in our grade wishes they were you, Alyssa, or Lisa?"

"Lisa has no parents; Alyssa just got dumped in front of an entire party; and I'm about to get grounded for a year," Cathy stated with a short laugh. "I'm sure we'd all gladly trade places with the majority of the girls in our grade."

Chantal raised her eyebrows. "Well, other people don't see it that way. They just see how pretty you are and how much the guys like you."

"Chantal, we're identical," Cathy laughed. "If people wish they were me, then they wish they were you, too. Lisa, Alyssa, and I don't care about what other people think of us."

"Well, Courtney cares—or did care. I don't know. Hopefully she'll make up with Marielle and Julianna," Chantal said.

"So, you have no idea how Jon ended up with Julianna this morning?" Cathy inquired.

Chantal shook her head. "They were there when I woke up. I'm sure I'll find out when I talk to Marielle later."

"Did Jon seem into Julianna?"

"He was certainly paying a lot of attention to her," Chantal replied. "I tried not to look at him. I talked mostly to Marc."

Cathy felt a slight pang of jealousy at the sound of her sister's words. "I know Marc."

"He's nice," Chantal said. "I can't believe I had never met him, considering all the time I used to spend at Chris's house in seventh grade."

"Well, he avoids Chris's house whenever Jordan's there," Cathy said. "He's been around a lot more since Jordan left for college."

"He kind of flirted with me," Chantal admitted. "I told him about Andy before it could get too far."

Again, Cathy felt a bit jealous. Evidently, she had developed a fondness for Marc. "I hung out with Marc on Wednesday night. He and I were partners in a game. I bet he felt comfortable with you because he knows me," Cathy said, feeling the need to lay claim to him.

"Probably," Chantal said. "He told me he's friends with Andy's brother. Andy didn't drink last night, right?"

Cathy shook her head. "Not a drop."

"He said he was going with Robby to pick up Robby's girlfriend before it got too rowdy," Chantal explained. "Robby was afraid the cops would show up because they showed up at Luke's last two parties."

"Well, he wasn't wrong," Cathy remarked. "Jason lives in too nice of a neighborhood for unruly parties. Evidently, his neighbors like to call the cops."

"I guess Marc and some of his friends avoided the scene altogether," Chantal said. "It's football season, so they can't risk getting in trouble. Matt must be full of regret."

Cathy took a deep breath. "I hope he's not in a lot of trouble. It wasn't his party."

"He still allowed it to happen."

"True... but Matt's a really good kid. He's nothing like Luke... or Jason."

"I've heard some disturbing things about Jay recently," Chantal commented and looked at Cathy apprehensively.

Cathy rolled her eyes. "Of course you have. Everyone loves to talk about him."

Chantal put her head down and hesitated slightly before saying, "What I've heard has been hard to swallow because I used to think Jay was the smartest kid I knew."

You and me both, Cathy thought. "Don't believe everything you hear," she said. "Rumors can cause a lot of damage."

Chantal looked up and locked eyes with Cathy. "Did Jay and Chris really trip on acid the night before school started?"

Cathy looked away from her sister. "How did you hear about that?"

"That's what Andy heard from Lisa," Chantal replied.

"Yeah, well, there's a reason I hung out with Marc instead of Jason that night," Cathy muttered.

"So, it's true?" Chantal asked sadly. "I'm sorry. That must be really hard to deal with."

Cathy took a deep breath. She was surprised that Chantal seemed to still care about her and Jason. "We got in a fight over it, so he promised he would never do it again."

"Good!" Chantal exclaimed. "LSD sounds pretty scary."

"Oh, it is. Please don't tell anyone Jason tried it."

"I won't," Chantal pledged. "Are you in trouble with the police?"

"No," Cathy replied and shook her head. "They could tell I was sober."

Chantal looked at her skeptically.

"You think we are a group of druggies, but we're not," Cathy said. "I'm sure Andy will tell you that he only saw Leslie, Jeff, and Jason drinking."

"Leslie irks me," Chantal admitted. "I swear she likes Andy."

"She's with Adam."

"So?"

"Well, your friends aren't like my friends, right?" Cathy questioned her. "They don't go after their friends' significant others, do they?"

Chantal shook her head. "Andy would never do that to me or Adam."

"Then don't worry about it," Cathy directed. "Do you know how many girls like my boyfriend?"

"See!" Chantal exclaimed. "You know Jay is popular!"

"Popular with girls—no one will deny that. He's not feeling so 'popular' right now. Courtney's not the only person Chris dumped yesterday."

Chantal raised her eyebrows. "Chris and Jay got in a fight?"

Cathy nodded. "Jay's a mess about it."

Chantal squinted in thought. "I wonder what's been going through Chris's head lately."

"I think he's broken and trying to pick up the pieces," Cathy speculated. "Is this Marielle girl straightedge?"

Chantal nodded.

"Good," Cathy stated. "That's what he needs."

"It's good to talk to you," Chantal admitted and smiled slightly. "I can't think of the last time we did this."

Cathy raised her eyebrows. "Well, you'll probably be the only person I'm allowed to talk to for quite a while. Mom and Dad are going to ground me forever."

Forever turned out to be one month of no phone, no hanging out with her friends after school, and no socializing on the weekends—basically house arrest. Only after Jason showed up at Cathy's home, apologizing for putting her in a bad situation, did Mr. and Mrs. Kagelli agree to allow him over on the weekends when they would be home to supervise their interactions. It was clear to Cathy that her parents had lost trust in her, and she wanted the chance to earn it back. However, it was going to be a lonely first month of high school for both her *and* Jason. With Cathy grounded from him during the week and Chris taking a hiatus, Jason essentially lost his two closest companions. Considering how upset he was about his fight with Chris and how quickly he tended to get bored, Cathy feared September could be disastrous for her boyfriend. She wasn't wrong.

CHAPTER 27

Six Months Later - Present Day - March 2018

WHEN JASON ARRIVED HOME from school that afternoon, he had one thing on his mind: restoring Cathy's reputation. He was shocked to discover that his friends all thought Cathy had intentionally caused Chantal and Jon's breakup. She was so misunderstood and maligned. He could not wait to talk to Chantal and finish explaining everything to her. The rift between the twins finally made sense to him after a year and a half of confusion.

Unfortunately, Jason knew defending Cathy would come at a cost, and he would likely lose Jon's friendship. He hoped Jon had matured enough to understand that Jason had only been trying to protect Chantal, but he had to brace himself for the worst.

He hesitated slightly before picking up his iPhone to call Jon. He knew it would be best if Jon heard the truth about his and Chantal's breakup from Jason. When Jon answered, Jason took a deep breath before beginning to speak. "I have a confession to make," he said downheartedly.

Jon laughed. "What are you talking about, guy?"

"Chantal never broke up with you," Jason replied.

"Oh, I know," Jon responded casually. "Chantal and I figured it out months ago. Cathy pretended to be Chantal and said I should date Alyssa. I stupidly took that as a breakup, lashed out at Chantal, and ruined our relationship. I'm lucky to be friends with her again."

"Wrong," Jason stated flatly. "Cathy never pretended to be Chantal. She was returning your call that day. She was being a supportive sister, trying to get you to realize the error of your ways. You mistook her voice for Chantal's and thought she broke up with you."

"What?!" Jon exclaimed with a short laugh. "Dude, Cathy's in your head. I can't believe she still owns you like this."

"Anderson, I know it's true because Cathy told me about the message she left you before you ever claimed Chantal broke up with you. Lisa and Cathy only figured out there was a miscommunication *after* Chris told us your side of the story—like, three months later. Cathy wanted to tell Chantal, but Lisa and I convinced her to keep quiet."

"What?!" Jon repeated.

"You weren't treating Chantal right, and we wanted to protect her from you. That's my confession. I'm sorry. I had no idea you thought Cathy pretended to be Chantal until I talked to Chantal this afternoon."

"Jay, I need to process what you just said and call you back," Jon responded. "I…I…I don't even know what to say right now."

"I get it, and I'm sorry," Jason said. "Really, I am. I know now that we should have let you and Chantal figure things out on your own."

"I might throw up after we get off the phone," Jon admitted.

Jason winced. "I'll be waiting to hear from you," he said before ending the call. Despite the fact that Jon had dated three girls since his breakup with Chantal, it was more than obvious that she still owned a large piece of his heart.

Next, Jason scrolled to Alyssa's name in his contacts to repeat the conversation.

"But why didn't Cathy support Chantal while Andy was in the hospital?" Alyssa asked after Jason explained the situation.

"Because she couldn't," Jason replied. "She had to do everything in her power not to fall apart."

"By getting drunk and letting Lisa spread rumors about you around our school?" Alyssa asked sarcastically.

"Lyss, there's a lot you don't know about stuff I got Cathy into last year," Jason said. "There's a reason why I want to mend things with her. After Chantal cut Cathy out of her life, Cathy started having terrible anxiety attacks. Instead of helping her figure out the cause, I fed her drugs."

"You or Luke?" Alyssa asked.

"Both of us," Jason replied. "It was my idea. I'm more to blame than my brother. I was trying to help her. I really was, but I gave her bad advice. You've seen the way mine and Chris's lives have changed this year. If I had known what I know now, I wouldn't have fed her pills that changed her personality."

"What the heck, Jay?" Alyssa asked in a frustrated tone. "You and Lisa let me lose Chantal's friendship for over a year?"

"To save her from Jon, yes."

"Wow. I see how low my happiness was on your priority list."

"We thought you would be okay. We didn't think you would ever date him! You guys were like siblings."

"When Jon visited Chantal while Andy was in the hospital, they 'figured out' Cathy pretended to be her, and she became friends with him again. He told her my side of the story, and she apologized to me the next day. I have hated Cathy since I found out 'the truth' in October. Now, you're telling me it was all a huge misunderstanding?"

"A ginormous one."

Alyssa scowled. "So, Chantal and I both shut Cathy out of our lives for no reason?"

"Yes. Cathy has no idea anyone thinks she pretended to be Chantal."

"Ugh. What a mess! Everyone thinks Cathy is a psycho."

"I know, and losing her friends just added to her anxiety and depression. I can't imagine the amount of pain I caused her when I broke up with her."

"But you didn't think she intentionally broke up Chantal and Jon, so what reason did you have for breaking up with her?"

Jason sighed. "She wasn't herself. She was acting cold and immoral. Like you said, she wasn't there for Chantal after Andy's accident. She used to be the most empathetic person I knew. The change in her was too much for me to handle. You must have noticed it; you were still friends with her when her personality started to change."

"Honestly, I assumed you were both on a bunch of drugs because you were both acting shady. Whether you realized it or not, we all knew you were snorting pills, so we figured she was doing the same. It made it easier for me to believe Cathy had pretended to be Chantal."

Jason had always found Alyssa easy to talk to, and for that reason, he felt comfortable confiding in her. "I got myself in a lot of trouble after Chris stopped being my friend. I was in a dark place for a few months and my behavior devastated Cathy," he confessed. "I had a lot of reasons for breaking up with her in November, but I've realized her personality change was a product of the drugs I gave her. Now I want to do for Cathy what Chris did for me; I want to help her find herself again."

"Have you talked to Cathy?" Alyssa asked. "Is she still on drugs? She's always with Luke, and my brother told me Luke's gotten into some bad stuff."

"I don't know where she's at," Jason admitted. "I left her high and dry to rot because I was a mess. Ask Lisa about Cathy. I'm sure she knows how she's doing."

"Lisa and I barely talk. After she defended Cathy, I got mad at her."

"Well, maybe it's time to forgive her?"

Alyssa sighed.

"I'm sorry we put you through this," Jason apologized. "After seeing the aftermath of everything, I'm sure Lisa's sorry, too."

"I'll give Lisa a call," Alyssa said. "How did Chantal take the news?"

"Not well," Jason replied. "I'm going to talk to her more about it later."

"And Jon?"

"Even worse—I probably won't hear from him for a while."

"He still loves her."

"I know."

"Thank God we broke up in September. I would have wasted so much time with him."

"I'm glad you see it that way."

"So far this year has been about blessings in disguise," Alyssa remarked. "Hopefully, Cathy gets a blessing soon."

CHAPTER 28

Wʜᴇɴ ᴄᴀᴛʜʏ ᴀɴᴅ ᴍᴀʀᴄ left Maggiano's, she was relieved that he did not enter Taylor's address in his GPS. Evidently, he knew Boston well enough to find Broadway Street without using navigation. However, Cathy planned to tell Marc the truth about her and Luke's afternoon as soon as they left Taylor's apartment. As they approached his neighborhood, her stomach twisted into knots.

"I think you should come inside with me," Marc said as they neared Taylor's condo. "What I have to tell him has to be said in private, but you can wait in another room. I don't like the idea of you waiting alone in my truck."

"Okay," Cathy agreed, wondering how Taylor would react to seeing her.

Five minutes later, Taylor looked stunned when he opened the door and saw her standing beside Marc. Without Marc noticing, Cathy shook her head to let him know she had not said anything. Taylor immediately looked relieved. "Come in," he said and stepped aside to let them into his foyer.

"This place is nice," Marc commented, "a bit of an upgrade from JP."

"Yeah, something like that," Taylor responded and led them into the living room. He sat down in his leather recliner and peered at Marc with a perplexed expression. "I'm happy you're here, but I'm a bit confused as to what brought this on."

"Why were you at Northeastern earlier?" Marc inquired.

"I'm trying to get my transcript in order so I can transfer somewhere," Taylor replied.

"Well, look into transferring somewhere in Massachusetts," Marc said dryly and took a deep breath, "because I don't think you'll be leaving the state any time soon."

Taylor raised his eyebrows in a perplexed manner. "What?"

"Can we talk in private?" Marc asked.

"Um, sure," Taylor said, appearing bewildered. "We can go up to my room. Cathy, feel free to put whatever you want on TV."

Marc's blue eyes widened. "You remember Cathy?"

Taylor's eyes also widened while Cathy's stomach dropped. Taylor glanced at her and then back at Marc. "Yeah," he replied assuredly, "but Luke's Instagram has helped revive my memory a bit."

"That kid hates having his picture taken, yet he posts everything online," Marc commented and stood up from the couch.

Cathy was thankful that Marc seemed to think nothing of Taylor's comment. After they left the room, Cathy put on the Bruins game. While reaching for the remote, she noticed the box in which Taylor kept his dab pen. *I wonder if this really is just weed oil,* she thought as she removed the vaporizer from the box. She glanced at it apprehensively, wanting to take a hit off of it but dreading the guilt she would feel. She had not ingested any form of marijuana since Marc told her in January that it bothered him. She put the pen back in the box and pushed it away from her. As tempted as she was to calm her anxiety, she knew the only real solution was to tell Marc the truth about her and Luke's afternoon. After much reflection, she had realized her chronic depression was a direct result of losing her relationships with Chantal, Alyssa, and Jason, but her anxiety was a product of something else: the penchant she had developed over the past two years for omitting information.

CHAPTER 29

Upstairs in taylor's bedroom, Marc handed his brother the black cell phone Detective Roth had given him. "What's this?" Taylor asked in confusion.

"At BC, I had the privilege of meeting Detective Roth of the BPD. He's a BC grad."

Taylor's throat instantly went dry.

"Evidently, they're investigating our family," Marc added.

"What?" Taylor asked, feeling immediately sick to his stomach.

"They think you're in danger," Marc replied and locked his eyes on Taylor. "He said they know you're clean and that you want 'out of the game.' They want to work out a deal with you to help you break away from your supplier."

Taylor widened his eyes. "What do you mean 'a deal'?"

Marc shrugged. "He said the less I know, the better, so I didn't ask many questions. The lead detective's number is in that phone. Detective Roth said you're likely being watched, so you can't use it in public or for any other calls. The point of my meeting today was to give me that phone so you could open a line of communication with the BPD. I bet they want your testimony."

"Donny would have me killed," Taylor said and shook his head. "I can't rat."

"I'm sure the cops have a plan."

"My supplier is connected to some *really* nasty people," Taylor stated with emphasis. "They wouldn't stop with me. If I ever ratted, they could come after you and Jordan, Mom and Dad. I'm stuck in this."

Marc's eyes widened. "So, that's why BC is cooperating with them," he muttered.

"The cops wouldn't discuss the details of the case with your coaches," Taylor assured him, "but if I were to stop selling drugs or to rat on my guy, you could be in danger."

"So, you still sell drugs?"

"I have to," Taylor replied honestly. "I got involved with the wrong people. I made them too much money. They're not going to let me off the hook unless I recruit someone else. I can't do that. I can't drag anyone else into this pitiful lifestyle."

"So, what's your plan?" Marc questioned him. "To sell drugs for the rest of your life?"

"I don't have a plan. I'm just praying for a miracle right now," Taylor admitted. "I know no way out of this."

"Well, maybe my meeting was an answer to your prayers," Marc said. "You should at least call and hear the guy out."

"I should get a lawyer," Taylor reasoned. "I don't want to say anything to incriminate myself."

"Wouldn't meeting with a lawyer look suspicious if you're being followed?"

Taylor let out a heavy breath and rested his head in his hands. "I should go home and talk to Dad. He'll know what to do. He has friends who are lawyers. Maybe one of them can meet me at our house."

"I never thought in a million years you would put our family in danger," Marc stated with a look of disbelief. "You were the favorite child, the perfect athlete, the straight-A student, the pinnacle of success. I cannot comprehend how a *pill* stole all that from you."

Taylor closed his eyes and let out a deep breath. "You and me, both," he said after opening his eyes. "It really is true what they say. You think that it will never happen to you, that you're just experimenting, and that you are strong enough to work and play hard. I had too much confidence in myself—false confidence, obviously. Everyone had built me up so much that I believed I was invincible. I had no idea what I was capable of doing. When you stormed out of my apartment months ago, I got a glimpse at who I had become. I thought I was a leader, but I was wrong. I no longer knew how to make Dad proud, and I couldn't stand it. Without football, I had no idea who I was, and instead of trying to find myself, I copped out and got high."

"When did you stop?" Marc asked.

"I haven't had an opiate in my system since the last time I saw you."

"When you snorted Xanax and Percocet to sleep?"

Taylor nodded.

"You scared me that day. I thought you had snorted heroin."

Taylor winced. "I've never touched heroin."

Marc let out a sigh of relief. "That day, you said you ran out of OCs, but I saw that you had a bunch of Percocet left. It's basically the same thing. What stopped you from snorting it?"

"When I ran out of OCs and started going through withdrawal, I realized I was addicted, and it scared me."

"You didn't know?" Marc asked.

Taylor shook his head. "Dude, drugs mess with your mind. I knew I had screwed up at school and ruined some of my relationships, but I had no idea I was physically dependent on anything."

"So, you stayed clean after I saw you?"

Taylor nodded.

"You suffered through days and days of withdrawal pains without going to rehab?"

"Weeks," Taylor admitted.

"What motivated you to do that?"

"Football and you," Taylor replied without a second thought.

Marc raised his eyebrows and peered at his brother in a perplexed manner. "What did I do?"

"You left."

Marc lowered his eyebrows. "Yeah, probably when you needed your family the most," he muttered.

"You did the right thing," Taylor assured him. "Losing our relationship is what I needed; it motivated me to face my problems."

"Are you still with Julie?" Marc asked.

Taylor shook his head. "She tried to be there for me, but I pushed her away. She didn't know I was dealing, and I felt like a scumbag for hiding it from her."

"That's too bad. Our whole family loves her."

"I do, too. She thought I was just depressed about not playing. She knows the truth now. After we broke up, she found out everything," Taylor explained. "There's no chance for us."

"I've seen drugs ruin a lot of relationships lately."

"Speaking of that... The last time you visited me, you mentioned that Luke was giving Jason pills. Is that still happening?" Taylor asked.

Marc shook his head. "Jay's fine," he replied. "He went through a short-lived phase with some stuff, but Chris helped him realize there was a better way to deal with pain."

Taylor sighed with relief. "Glad to hear. Chris seems to be doing great."

"Chris is doing awesome."

"Okay, I have to ask. What are you doing with Jason's ex-girlfriend?" Taylor questioned him. "She's what? A freshman?"

Marc took a deep breath. "Yeah, but she's old for her grade. She'll be sixteen in July," he replied.

"Marc, you're going off to college in less than six months," Taylor said matter-of-factly. "You're going to enter BC dating a sophomore in high school?"

Marc rolled his eyes. "I'll worry about that when the time comes. We're not boyfriend and girlfriend; we're just seeing each other. Although, I don't usually focus so much of my attention on one girl."

"So why her?"

"We get along great, and she hasn't pressured me to 'commit' to her... Plus, I want to keep her away from Jason because he got her into drugs."

"Is she clean?" Taylor asked.

Marc shrugged. "I honestly don't know."

"You've spent all this time with her, and you can't tell if she does drugs?"

Marc shook his head. "The only thing she's ever done around me is drink, but according to Chris, her drug of choice was Xanax. He said it changed her personality so much that Jason thought she had turned into a narcissist. I don't think he realized it was a side effect of the pills he was giving her."

"Do you feel like you're dating a narcissist?"

"No, but narcissists don't show their ugly side until they have people wrapped around their fingers."

"True."

"She's a hard one to crack," Marc admitted. "After a few months, I still can't tell if she actually likes me or if she just likes having my attention."

"Do you like her? Or are you with her to keep her from getting back together with Jason?"

"Both," Marc replied. "I'm trying to undo the damage Luke caused."

"According to Luke, he and Cathy spend a lot of time together," Taylor remarked. "He could still be giving her drugs. He still buys drugs from me, Marc."

Marc sighed. "I know, but I can't question him about it without admitting I know you're his dealer. I don't want that getting around Montgomery. No one knows Luke gets his stuff from you."

"Chris knows," Taylor retorted. "Other people must know."

Marc shook his head. "None of my friends know you sell to Luke. Very few people even know Luke deals. Matt thinks he just buys coke and molly off someone in Montgomery. Luke's done a good job at keeping things hush-hush."

"Well, that makes me feel a little better," Taylor admitted. "You didn't slander me, even though we were in a fight?"

"What good would that have done?" Marc asked rhetorically.

CHAPTER 30

CATHY LOCKED HER GREEN eyes on Marc's muscular body as he and Taylor entered the living room. She could not help but wonder what had been said during their private conversation in Taylor's bedroom. The dynamic between the brothers appeared to have improved since they went upstairs. This made Cathy happy, but she feared telling Marc about her previous visit to Taylor's condo with Luke would cause a problem. Nevertheless, for the sake of her own mental health, she had resolved to be honest with Marc. The idea of creating space between Marc and herself by withholding such information turned her stomach. She could not bear the thought of losing him, and this brought the realization that she might actually be falling in love with him.

"How's the game?" Marc asked while glancing from Cathy to the television.

"Scoreless," Cathy replied, hoping they would head to TD Garden soon.

"Glad we haven't missed any goals," Marc commented. "You ready to leave?"

Cathy nodded.

"All right. T? See you Sunday?" Marc questioned his brother. His words and warm tone took Cathy by surprise.

"Most likely," Taylor replied.

Marc gave Taylor a thumbs up sign and then nodded for Cathy to follow him to the door. After saying goodbye to Taylor, Cathy followed Marc down

Broadway Street until they reached his truck. She was debating over telling him about her afternoon visit with Taylor on the way to TD Garden or after the game. Assuming the news would upset him, she decided confiding in him afterward would be better.

CHAPTER 31

A S MARC LED CATHY toward section 324 of TD Garden, he felt happier than he had all year. Taylor was clean, and that meant more to him than he could possibly express in words. For over a year, Taylor had been the first person on Marc's mind when he woke up and the last person on his mind when he fell asleep. Although Marc knew Taylor was in a terrible predicament with his supplier and the police, he felt a remarkable sense of relief knowing he would not have to worry about his brother overdosing any longer. Marc had just spoken with *the real Taylor*. The driven and levelheaded leader Marc grew up admiring had been resurrected.

Marc's feelings of anger toward Taylor for selling drugs had dissolved. Taylor was not that person anymore; that person had been crucified through weeks and weeks of withdrawal pains. Was Taylor temporarily trapped in a rough situation and forced to sell drugs to stay alive? Yes. But was he happily selling drugs to teenagers? No.

For over a year, Marc had feared he would never have a conversation with *the real Taylor* ever again. Seeing him sober, alert, and motivated was the best sight in the world. Marc hoped he would join their family on Easter. Even more, he hoped Taylor would move back home. He felt certain that with his father's and the detectives' help, Taylor would be able to safely break free from his supplier.

"I love these seats!" Cathy exclaimed, stealing Marc away from his thoughts as they entered their row in the balcony. "Perfectly centered behind the Jumbotron—you never even have to turn your head to follow the puck. I'm so glad Luke was able to get us his family's season tickets."

Marc laughed. "For the balcony, they're great—and we didn't miss a goal." He placed his hand on Cathy's back as they made way to their seats.

Cathy turned and smiled at him before sitting down. Her green eyes sparkled, and she appeared far less anxious than she had earlier in the day.

"You look *very* happy," Marc commented as he sat down beside her.

"I am," Cathy remarked. "I miss coming to games."

"Oh, right. I'm sure Jay brought you a lot."

"A few times a year," Cathy replied. "But tonight, I'm happy to be here with you."

Marc smiled and put his arm around her. Then he pulled her close to his chest and kissed the top of her head. "I hope they win for you."

Cathy lifted her head and looked up at him adoringly. "I hope they win for both of us."

A few minutes later, Marc and Cathy were standing up in their seats, cheering to the Bruins goal song. At that moment, Marc felt more optimistic than he had in a long time.

GRIPPED PART 4 PREVIEW

March 2018

WITH A TWO-HOUR LAYOVER, Jordan Dunkin was sitting by the gate for his flight to Boston in Newark Liberty International Airport. He had opted to dive into some of his coursework for his Christian ethics class, while sipping on a Vanilla Bean Frappuccino. Jordan had signed up for the course to fulfill a core requirement, never imagining he would find the curriculum very interesting. However, he had quickly realized there was an immense amount of wisdom in what was being taught.

Prior to taking the course, Jordan was trying his best to become a better Catholic than he had been in high school. He wanted his family, coaches, and professors to take him seriously. After earning a starting spot on Notre Dame's football team and having a winning season, Jordan began to believe God was blessing him for the positive changes he was making to his lifestyle. When he ran into Michelle Taylor over Christmas break, she expressed interest in keeping in touch, which he took as a sign he was on the right path. His Christian ethics class gave him and Michelle a lot to discuss because she was a devout Christian with a sound understanding of the Bible. She had a knack for explaining things in a way that made sense to Jordan, and he found himself growing more and more interested in not only Michelle, but also the things of God. He finally desired to have the type of relationship with Christ that his father had been talking about for years.

Jordan noticed that the more deeply he dove into the curriculum, the more his perspective on life was changing. One year prior, he never would have passed up on a spring break trip to the Caribbean to go home. Now, he was excited to spend a week in Montgomery with his family. He specifically wanted to uncover what was going on in his older brother Taylor's life. Taylor, who had once been Jordan's greatest role model, had been struggling with a painkiller addiction for over a year. Although Jordan was doing everything in his power to avoid following his older brother's footsteps, he respected the leader Taylor had once been and hoped that person still existed somewhere inside of him.

It had been like a dream to attend Montgomery Lake High as Taylor Dunkin's younger brother. Taylor had paved the way for Jordan to have great success on the football field without much effort. Making varsity as a freshman was unheard of, but Taylor made it happen for Jordan. Of course, as Captain, Taylor trained Jordan harder than anyone else on the team, making sure he was an effective receiver. Taylor and Jordan grew up playing catch together in their backyard, so the connection they shared on the field was unprecedented. As a freshman, Jordan became the number one targeted receiver, and MLH had an undefeated season. The opportunity that Taylor gave Jordan to shine led to numerous recruiters contacting him—albeit illegally—well before his junior year of high school.

It honestly felt wrong to attend Notre Dame without Taylor. It was the university Taylor had chosen over Vanderbilt, Auburn, USC, 'Bama, BC, Northeastern, Clemson, The U, and Penn. At the time, Taylor and Jordan had dreamed of playing on the same team again, and that had motivated Jordan to focus in school. When Taylor lost his chance with Notre Dame—due to an arrest after a supposed senior-prank-gone-wrong—Jordan assumed Taylor would, at the very least, try to transfer there in the future. He never expected Taylor to settle for playing on an unranked team. When Taylor opted not to transfer as a sophomore, Jordan grew concerned about his brother's mental health.

It became apparent that losing his chance to play for a ranked team had taken some wind out of Taylor's sails. His arrest had been unfortunate because it was completely out of character for Taylor to participate in any sort of prank. The news had completely shocked Jordan, who had always considered his older brother a bit uptight. Moreover, it shook the bottoms off their parents and teachers. Jordan honestly believed that if Taylor had never been arrested, his current situation would have been very different. He assumed the resulting failure and embarrassment Taylor felt was what drove him to begin experimenting with recreational drugs in college. While most people blamed Taylor's painkiller addiction on his knee injury, Jordan believed Taylor's 2013 senior-prank-gone-wrong was the root cause.

Jordan's cell phone vibrated on his lap, pulling his attention away from his ethics book. He smiled when he saw a text from Michelle on the screen. Sliding her message open, he read:

Michelle: *When do you land in Boston? I'm in the Seaport now with my friends. You won't believe it, but I ran into Taylor at Northeastern today.*

Jordan: *I hope you're still pulling for ND after your tour today!*

Michelle: *For sure!!*

Jordan: ☺ *I land around 10. My parents are picking me up. Otherwise I would take an Uber and meet you in the Seaport. How did Taylor look?*

Michelle: *Oh bummer... are we still good for tomorrow? Taylor looked and sounded great.*

Jordan: *We are most definitely good for tomorrow. I'm going to head into the city to visit T in the morning and then I'm all yours.*

Michelle: ☺ *Will you text me after you land in Boston safely?*

Jordan: *Sure thing*

Michelle: *Praying you have a safe flight!*

Jordan: *Thanks. Have fun tonight!*

Jordan smiled as he set his phone down on his lap. He felt incredibly blessed to have Michelle back in his life. She had first caught his eye when he was a junior and she was a freshman in high school. Of course, at the time, he had been too immature to appreciate her inherent goodness or purity. In fact, during his senior year, he had foolishly told his younger brother Marc that he planned to take Michelle's virginity, which was most likely why Marc erroneously believed Jordan had slipped something into Michelle's drink at a party. While home for spring break, Jordan hoped to set the record straight with Marc. The secret of what really happened that night had been concealed for over two years, and it was time for the truth to be told.

CHECK OUT THE REST OF THE GRIPPED SERIES

Gripped Part 1: The Truth We Never Told

In high school, Taylor Dunkin broke more records than any other athlete to step foot in Montgomery, Massachusetts. As a sophomore in college, he was ranked by ESPN as one of the NFL's top 100 prospects. However, his aspirations came to a jarring halt when a season-ending injury sent him spiraling into a dark world of pain, depression, and addiction.

One year later, Taylor is a person of interest in a highly confidential investigation headed by the Boston Police Department. He has entangled himself in a crime ring notorious for pushing drugs on local college campuses. Montgomery's hometown hero has fallen hard, and he's taking a lot of people down with him.

Luke Davids has become the middleman between Taylor and teens in Montgomery who want to buy drugs. Freshmen Cathy Kagelli, Chris Dunkin, and Jason Davids are just a few of the students at Montgomery Lake High who have fallen victim to the benzos and opiates supplied by Taylor and Luke.

When Taylor's youngest brother Marc discovers that Taylor is behind the copious amount of pills circulating around his high school, he sets off to not only reverse the damage Taylor has caused, but also save his lifelong role model from becoming a casualty of America's deadly opioid epidemic.

Gripped Part 2: Blindsided

Fourteen-year-old Chris Dunkin is known for being the life of the party and everyone's favorite friend. Despite his amicable nature, he carries around deep-seated pain from his childhood that he frequently numbs with alcohol and drugs.

After hosting a party, Chris awakes with a strange vibe

running through his body and no recollection of the previous night. When he learns the horrifying truth of what his night entailed, the trajectory of his life is changed forever.

Gripped Part 4: Smoke & Mirrors

After spending her first month of high school grounded, Cathy Kagelli is finally allowed to socialize and uncover what her boyfriend, Jason Davids, has been up to without her. When Cathy realizes Jason has been experimenting with a variety of drugs, she devises a plan to save him from himself... but she just may lose herself in the process.

Meanwhile Taylor Dunkin finds himself playing a game with even higher stakes because his life, his reputation, and the safety of everyone he loves are all on the line. Taylor's two younger brothers, Jordan and Marc, have been at odds for years, but they are brought together to decipher the mysterious clues Taylor is leaving regarding his whereabouts. As secrets are revealed, the Dunkin boys' relationships will be changed forever. In Taylor's weakest moment, he made a deal with the devil, and now there is a reckoning. But who will pay the price?

Gripped Part 5: Taylor's Story
Taylor Dunkin is missing.

The last message Jordan Dunkin receives from Taylor leads him to Taylor's abandoned Jeep. Each of Taylor's family members holds a piece of the puzzle, and as the Dunkins begin putting the details together, they are awakened to the possibility they may never see Taylor again.
No one can find Missy Kent.

Missy's boyfriend Luke Davids last saw her dancing with their friends at a nightclub, but she hasn't responded to anyone's texts or calls for hours.
Everything is connected.

Taylor and Missy's friends are dangerously close to learning the truth, but their ignorance might be the only thing keeping them safe. Every clue is leading them closer to peril.

The fifth book in the Gripped series moves through details at a thrilling pace. Secrets are revealed and lives are at stake. Taylor, Missy, their friends, and their families must figure out who they can trust before it's too late.

IF YOU ENJOYED *GRIPPED*, CHECK OUT MONTGOMERY LAKE HIGH

Montgomery Lake High #1: The Right Person

Growing up in the shadow of two NFL-destined cousins, Chris Dunkin has high hopes for his own future in football. However, a drug addiction threatens to destroy everything he has worked hard to attain. When Chris meets Courtney Angeletti—the mayor's straightedge Christian daughter—he believes she could be the source of inspiration he needs to overcome his destructive lifestyle. Courtney, however, has other ideas.

The desire to rebel has been tugging on Courtney's heartstrings for some time, and Chris's "bad-boy" reputation draws her to him like a moth to a flame. After all, he is a central part of the most popular clique in her high school. Will Chris pull Courtney away from her faith or will Courtney inspire him to overcome his rebellious lifestyle?

Montgomery Lake High #2: When Darkness Tries to Hide

Students at Montgomery Lake High believe the ominous clouds and impending storm will only bring a temporary interruption to their regularly scheduled lives. However, when the tempest grows worse and a classmate's life hangs in the balance, students must pull together to support each other and seek help for their friend. As the lines between cliques dissolve, dark secrets are revealed and hearts are transformed.

Montgomery Lake High #3: The Aftermath

At age fifteen, Jason Davids appears to have it all: high grades, popular friends, a beautiful girlfriend, and nearly any worldly thing that promises enjoyment at his disposal. Despite this, there is a persistent emptiness inside his heart. After failing to fill the void with achievements, relationships, and illicit substances, Jason finds himself intrigued by Jessie: a rather quiet girl, who is the daughter of a local pastor. How is it possible that she stands for everything his lifestyle opposes yet possesses the one thing he has been searching for all along?

Montgomery Lake High #4: The Battle for Innocence

Jon Anderson and Chantal Kagelli are trying to live moral lives, but temptations are plaguing them in and out of school. Will they continue to be lights in their best friends' lives or will they get pulled into the darkness?

Montgomery Lake High #5: The Forces Within

After being trapped inside his own body, unable to communicate with anyone but his own thoughts, Andy Rosetti finally wakes up from the coma that controlled his life for one month. But upon awakening, Andy finds himself and his friends in an unfamiliar setting: a mansion riddled with secret passages and supernatural forces. As his friends fall prey to the entities surrounding them, Andy must figure out if the darkness lies within the mansion's walls or within the people surrounding him.

ABOUT THE AUTHOR

College counselor, award-winning author, and entrepreneur Stacy Padula of Plymouth, Massachusetts has accrued years of experience working with adolescents as an educational consultant, as well as a mentor, life coach, and youth group leader. She is the author of eleven Young Adult novels. Her first novel, "The Right Person," was published in 2010. In 2011, "When Darkness Tries to Hide" was published, and it was followed by "The Aftermath" in 2013. In 2014, both "The Battle for Innocence" and "The Forces Within" were released, and in 2015, all five books hit the shelves of Barnes & Noble. For Stacy, it was a dream come true to see her books for sale in the popular, mainstream bookstore! In 2016, Barnes & Noble chose Stacy to be a featured author for its teen book festival. In 2019, she released a new book series titled "Gripped," that takes place in the same "world" as Montgomery Lake High but focuses on different main characters. "Gripped Part 1: The Truth We Never Told" was released in February 2019, and "Gripped Part 2: Blindsided" was released in July 2019. "Gripped Part 3: The Fallout" was released in November 2019, and "Gripped Part 4: Smoke & Mirrors" was released in May 2020. In 2019, Stacy Padula also wrote her first screenplay, an adaptation of her novel "The Aftermath" and worked on writing a pilot for "Gripped" which caught the attention of Hollywood producers. The "Gripped" series is currently being adapted for TV by Emmy-winning producer Mark Blutman. In 2020, Stacy began writing a third book series with NBA Coach Brett Gunning. Geared towards children ages three through eight, Stacy and Brett's soon-to-be-released "On The Right Path" book series has been endorsed by Joel Osteen, Mike D'Antoni, and Kevin McHale as a series that belongs in every school, library, and household.

Stacy was featured in Marquis Who's Who in America (2018, 2019, & 2020) for excellence in literature and education, Marquis Who's Who in the World (2018, 2019, & 2020), and Cambridge Who's Who for Young Professionals (2009). In 2018, she was awarded the Albert Nelson Lifetime

Achievement Award, and in 2019, the International Association of Top Professionals (IAOTP of New York, NY) chose Stacy Padula as its "Top Educational Consultant of the Year." Then in 2020, she was named "Empowered Woman of the Year" by IAOTP. Each of her novels have risen to best seller status in a variety of categories on Amazon from 2010-Present. From February through March of 2019, "Gripped Part 1" was the #1 New Release on Amazon Kindle in its category. In November of 2019, "Gripped Part 3" was the #1 New Release on Amazon in Paperback and on Kindle in 3 different genres. In May and June of 2020, "Gripped Part 4" became the #1 New Release on Amazon in multiple genres as well. In November of 2020, Stacy was named a "Social Impact Hero" by Authority Magazine for her support of animal rescues through her publishing company. That month, she was also chosen to be featured on the cover of T.I.P. Magazine, an international business publication. In April of 2021, "On The Right Path" because the #1 New Release on Amazon in its genre. In June of 2021, Stacy was featured on the famous Reuters Building in Times Square as Empowered Woman of the Year.

Background: Stacy grew up in Pembroke, Massachusetts and graduated from Silver Lake Regional High School. She was a Presidential Scholar and on the Dean's List at Wentworth, where she studied Architectural Engineering and Interior Design. After graduation, she worked at an architecture firm in Boston from 2006-2008. Although she enjoyed her work, she felt something was missing-she wanted to spend more time helping people grow academically, personally, and spiritually. For close to a year, she split her time between tutoring, writing, and working at a design firm in Plymouth. When she fell in love with tutoring, she left the A&D industry completely and took a full-time position with a private education company in Dover, Massachusetts. She attained tutoring certification in 2009 through The International Tutor Association. Her career took off, and within one year, she was promoted to Director. Stacy knew she had found her niche! During her eight years with that company, she received multiple promotions and held a variety of titles, including Manager of Curriculum & Instruction and Director of Operations. In 2016, Stacy founded South Shore College Consulting & Tutoring. Then in 2019, she founded

Briley & Baxter Publications—a publishing company that uses part of its monthly proceeds to support animal rescues. Stacy is currently enrolled in the University of Pennsylvania Wharton School's online Entrepreneurship Specialization to pursue her passion for business. In her spare time, she enjoys skiing, taking online classes, following the stock market, attending Bruins games, playing fantasy sports, reading about psychology, hosting Bible studies, taking her dogs to the beach, and spending time with her family, husband Tim, and friends.

CONNECT WITH US!

Stacy's Instagram @author_stacypadula
Stacy's Twitter @thegrippedbooks
Cathy's Instagram @ckagelli99
Chantal's Instagram @chantal_kagelli
Jason's Instagram @jds_on
Lisa's Instagram @lisa_ankerman99
Chris's Instagram @dunkin_85
Luke's Instagram @lukedavids97
Alyssa's Instagram @alyssa_kelly02
www.stacyapadula.com
www.brileybaxterbooks.com
www.highambition.org

Did You Enjoy Gripped Part 3?
If you loved this book, would you please leave a review on Amazon?